HER OUTBACK
COMMANDER

HER OUTBACK COMMANDER

BY

MARGARET WAY

First published in Great Britain 2011
by Mills & Boon, an imprint of Harlequin (UK) Limited.
Large Print edition 2011
Harlequin (UK) Limited, Eton House,
18-24 Paradise Road, Richmond, Surrey TW9 1SR

© Margaret Way, Pty., Ltd 2011

ISBN: 978 0 263 22244 9

Harlequin (UK) policy is to use papers that are natural,
renewable and recyclable products and made from
wood grown in sustainable forests. The logging and
manufacturing process conform to the legal environmental
regulations of the country of origin.

Printed and bound in Great Britain
by CPI Antony Rowe, Chippenham, Wiltshire

CHAPTER ONE

Vancouver
Canada

HE KNEW her the moment she moved into the hotel lobby. The doorman in his natty top hat held the door for her, his face wreathed in smiles. Who could blame him? A woman like that inspired smiles. But just why he was so sure it was *she* he couldn't fathom. Gut feeling? He didn't question it, even when it went against all his preconceptions. But then his mental picture had been based on the description Mark had given his mother, Hilary, in a one-off letter sent months after he had married the Canadian girl. Nevertheless the feeling of recognition was so powerful it was almost a force in itself. It shook him when he was a man who shielded himself against shock.

For one thing, Mark's description didn't begin to do her justice. She was *beautiful*. No other word would do. She always would be, given her bone structure, he thought. She also radiated an air of refinement—a cool reserve that in itself was unusual. Not Mark's scene at all. She was immaculately groomed, her stylishness understated. She was a recent widow, after all, he thought grimly. Obviously her lovely outward appearance camouflaged the shallowness of the woman beneath.

He had chosen the most inconspicuous spot he could find to wait for her. He reasoned it would give him a slight advantage, observing her before she had a chance to observe him. That way he might be able to form a better idea of what sort of young woman Mark had married. Right now he found himself unable to grasp the reality when set against his half brother's description. Where, for instance, was the blonde hair? And surely she was supposed to be petite? But then she was wearing high heels, and women moved on, changing their hair colour as fashion or mood dictated.

He knew in his bones he hadn't picked the wrong woman, despite the many discrepancies. He was supposed to keep an open mind. This had to be Mandy—Mark's widow, Amanda. She didn't look like a Mandy, or even an Amanda.

Pretty names, but they didn't suit her. Perhaps it was one of Mark's little jokes? From boyhood Mark had revelled in deception, spinning an elaborate web of fantasies, half-truths and shameless lies that had tied everyone in knots. Their father had once confided he was worried Mark was becoming something of a sociopath. A harsh judgement when their father hadn't been a judgemental man. But it had to be admitted Mark had barely registered the difference between right and wrong. Nothing had stopped him when his mind was set on something. He certainly hadn't *cared* about people. His self-interest had been profound. That hadn't been an easy truth for either his father or him to accept.

As for his tastes in young women? Mark had only been interested in pretty girls who had all their assets on show. Other qualities a young woman might offer, like warmth, companionship, spirituality or intellect, came right down the list. Mark's type had always been the stereotypical glamour girl. "Air-heads" Marcia, his twin, had always called them acidly, with the exception of Joanne Barrett, the fiancée Hilary had picked out for her son and whom Mark had so callously abandoned. This woman he had finally chosen to marry presented a striking departure from the norm.

As she stood poised a moment, looking about her, he rose to his feet to hold up an identifying hand. Poor Joanne wouldn't have been in the race beside this young woman, he thought, with regret mixed with resentment. There was no comparison. At least in the looks department.

No welcoming smile appeared on her face.

Nor on his.

His heart was locked against her like cold steel.

She walked towards him, a willowy figure, glancing neither to left nor right. She seemed to have little idea of the admiring glances she was receiving, from men and women alike. But then a beautiful woman would never escape constant attention. She was probably so used to it she didn't notice.

His trip to Vancouver, beautiful city though it was, surrounded by mountains and sea, unfortunately wouldn't entail pleasure, or even time for some sightseeing. He regretted that. But he would have to say he wasn't at home in such cold—let alone the rain. Outside the centrally heated hotel it was *freezing*, with a biting wind. He had never known it to be so cold, even when wintering in Europe. He had been born and raised on a vast Australian cattle station on the fringe of one of the world's great deserts, the scorching blood-red Simpson. But he was here for a specific purpose: to arrange for his half-brother's body to be taken home and to invite Mark's widow to return with him to Australia, to attend the funeral and finally meet the family. The family she had chosen to totally ignore for the two short years of her marriage.

He didn't think she would ignore them now. There was a sizable legacy he wished to give her, for a start. Very few people knocked back money. Besides, a few deserving people had a right to know why Mark had acted the way he had. First and foremost his mother Hilary, his twin Marcia, and the cruelly jilted Joanne. *He* needed no explanations. Mark's actions had *never* shocked him. And they had never shocked their late father, who had spent the last two years of his life as an invalid, his spine fractured so badly that two operations hadn't helped at all. The titanium pins simply hadn't been able to hold. To make matters so much more devastating, their father had suffered a rare type of amnesia since his near fatal accident. He remembered nothing of the day when he, a splendid horseman, born in the saddle, had been thrown violently from his favourite mare Duchess.

She walked towards him quite calmly, when inside she was anything but calm. This was Blaine Kilcullen. Mark's brother. She would have recognised him even if he hadn't raised that signalling hand. It was an authoritative hand—the hand of a man well used to getting instant attention. Yet the gesture didn't strike her as arrogant. More a natural air of command. He was very tall. Much taller than Mark. Six-three, she guessed, with wide square shoulders, long lean limbs. Superbly fit. He cut an impressive figure. But then Lucifer had been a splendid angel before the Fall.

Memories shunted into her mind: Mark's damning condemnation of his brother.

Handsome as Lucifer and just as deadly.

It had been delivered with a kind of primal anger, even hate. Mark had had a big problem with anger, she remembered. Indeed there had been quite a few aspects of Mark's personality she had found jarring, and had done so right from the start. Charming one minute, and within the space of another he could turn oddly cold, as if the shutters had come down. Impossible to pinpoint the exact reason for the abrupt change.

Mark had claimed his brother was the cause of so much of the unhappiness and pain in his life. He might well have contributed, she reasoned, given the strength of Mark's bitterness and his sense of abandonment.

"Blaine is the reason I had to get away. Leave my home, my own country. My dad died, but long before he died he rejected me—because of Blaine and his manipulative ways. Blaine was out to eliminate me and he did it in the worst possible way. He bitterly resented Dad's love for me. In the end Dad pushed me away. I was never good enough. I could never measure up. Snow will blanket the Simpson before I speak to my brother again."

Alas, Mark had got his wish. At least in part. He *had* been fated never to speak to his brother again. He had died in snow. A skiing accident after he had, despite warnings, left the trail they had been taking and not long after crashed headlong into a tree. She and Amanda had been watching at the time. It had been a horrible experience, one that could never be forgotten. But Mark had enjoyed playing the daredevil, like some macho adolescent. Perhaps his former life, the never-ending efforts to prove himself against a superior brother, had dictated his attitude? At times she'd had the awful dread he might be borderline suicidal. He'd definitely had issues. But then she had managed to convince herself she was most likely overreacting. She was no psychiatrist, after all.

"Amanda?" The cattle baron extended a lean, darkly tanned hand.

Time for her to unfold another one of Mandy's stories. She had spent so many years covering for her cousin she was starting to feel drained.

"I'm so sorry, Mr Kilcullen." His handshake was firm, brief, but she felt a very real *frisson* of reaction—a kind of shock wave produced by skin on skin. She tried to hide her involuntary reaction, launching into an explanation. "There wasn't time to let you know, I'm afraid. I'm Sienna Fleury, Amanda's cousin. Amanda asked me to take her place. A migraine. It came on quite suddenly. She suffers from them."

"I see."

Exquisitely polite. But she had no difficulty reading his mind. More cold indifference from the woman Mark had married. More rejection of the Kilcullen family of him as the family envoy.

"Please allow me to offer my most sincere condolences." She spoke gently. "I was fond of Mark." It was far from the truth, but then it never did seem right to speak ill of the dead. At the beginning she had made a super-human effort to like Mark, but there had always been something in his eyes that disturbed her. Amanda, however, had fallen madly in love with him, so in rejecting Mark the family had known it would be as good as rejecting Amanda. Something she could not do, having looked out for Amanda for years like a surrogate big sister.

"Thank you, Ms Fleury." He felt his grim mood softened by her lovely speaking voice. The musical Canadian accent fell soothingly on his ear. Looking back at her, he felt something click in his mind, pretty much as if a light switch had been turned on. Hadn't Amanda's *bridesmaid* featured quite a bit in Mark's letter to his mother? At the time Hilary had confessed she found the talk of the bridesmaid quite odd. Could *this* be the anonymous bridesmaid? From believing she was Mark's widow, he was now convinced she could be Amanda's bridesmaid.

Sienna, quietly observing him, detected the shift in his attitude. She wondered what had caused it. From Mark's account the brothers had been mortal enemies. Believing her husband implicitly, Amanda had made no effort to contact her late husband's estranged family, no effort to effect some sort of reconciliation. She had even been obdurate in not wanting to advise them of Mark's fatal accident. But that had been against the right code of behaviour. Sienna had contacted her father, Lucien Fleury, one of Canada's most highly esteemed artists, and begged him to make the call as Amanda couldn't or wouldn't.

"Always been problematic, hasn't she? Poor little Mandy." An understatement from her father, who rarely bothered to mince words.

Amanda was his niece. His sister Corinne and her husband had been killed in a car crash when Amanda was five. Sienna's parents, Lucien and

Francine, had taken in the orphaned Amanda, raising her with Sienna, eighteen months older, and Sienna's adored older brother Emile, now a brilliant architect and interior designer working out of New York.

Blaine Kilcullen's deep voice, with its clear cutting edge, broke into her thoughts. No discernible Aussie accent. More a cosmopolitan voice. "Shall we have a drink before dinner?" he suggested, his diamond gaze revealing nothing of what he thought of her and her unheralded role as stand-in for his half-brother's widow.

"I'd like that." What else could she say? She actually found him every bit as daunting as Mark had said. But then she had to give him a little leeway. These were unhappy times.

Inside the luxurious lounge, he helped her remove her cashmere coat, laying it over the back of a chair along with the deep yellow scarf she had worn around her throat. It was quite a while since she had been inside this downtown Vancouver boutique hotel. She glanced appreciatively around her. The hotel was famous for its European style: glossy, warm dark timbers, richly upholstered furniture, fine antique pieces, lots of lovely flowers, and beautiful works of art that adorned the public areas as well as the luxurious suites.

He held her chair. She sat down, smoothing back the long hair that had been caught into her woollen scarf.

"What would you like?" He diverted his gaze from the shining waterfall of hair, turning his attention to the ceiling-high, well-stocked bar.

"Perhaps a brandy cocktail?" She didn't really want anything.

He settled for a fine cognac.

Careful not to stare, she was nevertheless making her own assessment with her artist's eye. At twenty-six she already had several successful art showings behind her. She was also a talented photographer, with a good body of work. Her primary job, however, was managing her father's gallery in Vancouver, and overseeing two others—one in Toronto, the other in New York. What was her take on the man in front of her? Blaine Kilcullen, Australian cattle baron, was without a doubt the most striking-looking man she had ever seen, even allowing for the severe expression on his handsome face. But then he would be in mourning for his brother. Bitter regrets, surely? Thoughts of "what might have been"?

He was wearing a beautifully tailored dark suit with a silk tie she very much liked: wide cobalt blue and silver stripes, the blue edged with a fine line of dark red. He would probably look just as elegant in traditional cattleman's gear, she thought. The leanness and the long limbs made an ideal frame for clothes. The surprising thing was the Mark hadn't resembled his brother in the least. Mark had had golden-brown hair and mahogany dark eyes, and he'd been around five-ten. This man was darkly handsome. His thick hair had a natural deep wave, and his strongly marked brows were ink-black. In stunning contrast his eyes had the glitter of sun on ice.

Their drinks arrived. She readied herself for what was to come. Conversation would be difficult. The great irony was that it wasn't her affair at all. *Amanda* was Mark's widow. It was *Amanda's* place to attend this crucial meeting with a member of Mark's family, albeit estranged. Only Amanda had pulled the old hysteria trick. Over the years she had turned it into an art form.

The sad fact of the matter was Amanda really could make herself ill, thus giving her the upper hand. They had all bowed to her tantrums, acutely sympathetic to the fact she had lost her parents, but by the time she'd reached her teens it had become apparent that Amanda actually enjoyed wallowing in her feelings. Earlier in the day she had maintained, with tears gushing, she couldn't *possibly* meet Mark's cruel, callous brother.

"We're talking about the brother who tried to wreck his life, Sienna. You expect me to head off to a pow-wow, smoke the peace pipe? Not likely!"

Mark had impressed upon Amanda and the family that he had *hated* his brother, blaming him for his banishment from the Kilcullen ancestral home—although he had been very sketchy about that. It was a desert fortress, apparently, set down in the middle of nowhere. She had checked the Simpson area out on the internet, reading about the breathtaking changes that occurred in the wilderness after rain. It sounded quite fascinating.

Mark had thought differently. "Canada suits me fine. God knows it's far enough away—the other side of the world." From time to time there had been such abrupt surges of anger, amounting to rants, flushed skin, darting eyes. She'd once suggested Mark might need professional help to Amanda, falling back defensively against Amanda's hysterical tirade.

"How dare you? Dare you? Dare you?"

Sienna had never mentioned it again.

The odd thing was Mark hadn't met Amanda in their home city of Vancouver. He had met her when she and Amanda were holidaying in Paris. Mark had been working behind the bar of their luxury hotel at the time.

"Just a fun job, and I get to meet all the beautiful girls."

Mark had lived for fun, taking casual jobs here and there in the hospitality industry where—surprisingly—he had shone. But then Mark had been physically a very attractive man. Only he had committed to nothing. Amanda was a born flirt, who'd had a succession of boyfriends, but she had fallen for him good and hard—and in a remarkably short time. As for Sienna herself, the sensible one, she hadn't taken to Mark—despite his good-looks and superficial charm. But he'd been the type Amanda had always been attracted to.

It hadn't come as much of a surprise when Mark had followed them home less than a month later. He'd met the family, who had recognised an imbalance there, but felt compelled for Amanda's sake to be tolerant. Amanda paid attention to no one, but in retrospect it would have been an excellent idea for her to listen. She would have no other. Within six months she and Mark had been married, at a small but lavish affair Lucien had turned on for them. There had been no one on Mark's side, although there had been a goodly sprinkling of Fleurys and friends to swell the numbers and make an occasion of it. It had later been revealed Amanda had been pregnant the time—something she had kept from them—but sadly she had miscarried barely a month later. She had not fallen pregnant again for the remainder of their short and, as it had turned out, largely unhappy marriage.

Sienna had often wondered if that was the reason Mark had married Amanda—although to be fair Amanda was very pretty and she could be good company when the mood took her. It had never seemed to Sienna that Mark had been in love with her cousin. Using her, maybe? Their

family was wealthy. Her father was an eminent
artist, her mother a dermatologist and her brother
was becoming quite a celebrity designer. For that
matter she was doing pretty well herself. Only
Mark had never seemed short of money. He'd
appeared to have private means. The jobs he'd
taken had seemed to be no more than hobbies.
At one time he had tried to talk her into allowing him to join her at the gallery. No question of
that. She hadn't wanted Mark anywhere near her.
He made her very uneasy. Barely a year into the
marriage Mark had finally shown her why. She
couldn't bear to think about that awful, shameful
evening. It still haunted her. From that night on
she had *loathed* him…

Blaine Kilcullen was speaking, drawing her out
of her dark, disturbing thoughts. "I do hope your
cousin is well enough to speak to me tomorrow,
Ms Fleury. I need to see her."

"Of course you do," she hastily agreed, thinking there would be world peace before Amanda
got out of bed.

"What is the real reason for her not coming,
Ms Fleury?"

"Please—Sienna." She took a sip of her cocktail. It perturbed her, the effect this man was having on her. It was as if he had a magnetic power. She was usually composed. Or that was her reputation. Amanda was the bubbly one. At least before her brief marriage had started to disintegrate.

"Sienna it is." He smiled briefly. That was enough. The smile lit the sombreness of his expression like an emerging sun cut through clouds. "Sienna—a significant name. Was it inspired by the colour of your hair?" He let his eyes linger on her long, lustrous mane. It was centre-parted no doubt to highlight the perfect symmetry of her oval face. The colour was striking: a blend of dark red, amber and coppery-brown. Her large beautiful eyes were thickly lashed. The colour put him in mind of fine sherry when held up to the light.

"My father named me," she said, a smile playing around her mouth. "Apparently even as a newborn my fuzz of hair was the colour of burnt sienna. That's a paint pigment. My father is quite a famous artist here in Canada. Lucien Fleury." She spoke with love and pride.

"It was *your* father, then, who rang Mark's mother to let her know of the accident?" Things were starting to fall into place.

Mark's mother. Why not *our* mother? "Yes, Amanda was so distraught she had to be sedated." Not true. Amanda had been drunk. Another cover-up. Amanda had taken to alcohol big-time.

"I feel I should see your father's work," he said, surprising her. "My family have been great collectors over the years. I have a great-aunt—Adeline—living in Melbourne, whose house is like a private museum. Paintings, sculptures, antiques, Oriental rugs, the most exquisite Chinese porcelains behind glass. She tells me every time she sees me she's leaving me the lot."

"Does that please you?" He was a cattle baron, a man of action, of the Great Outdoors, though his whole persona was that of a cultured man of the world. "Not everyone likes such things." She had friends who had little taste for art and antiques though they had the money to possess both.

His handsome mouth was compressed. A sexy mouth, very clean cut, its edges raised. She knew he wasn't married. That had emerged during the course of the conversation between Mrs Hilary

Kilcullen and her father. "In my case, I do. But God knows where it will all go. My current plan is to give the lesser stuff away. There's quite a large extended family. But you wouldn't know about that."

"Unfortunately, no." She lowered her gaze. "I should point out it's *Amanda* who is your brother's widow."

"Half-brother," he corrected a shade curtly, again surprising her. Mark had never said. "My mother died of the complications of malaria when I was going on six years of age. She and my father were staying at a friend's coffee plantation in New Guinea at the time. Both of them had had their shots, but in my mother's case the vaccine didn't take. My father, our New Guinea friends, the entire family were devastated by the loss. I still remember my beautiful mother, though those memories have kept changing over time. Hard to forget what she looked like, however. My father commissioned a large portrait of her by a famous Italian artist to celebrate their marriage. It hung in the Great Room. It never came down."

Not even when the second wife, Mark's mother, took her place? That couldn't have been easy for

Hilary Kilcullen. Come to that, this cattle baron himself was eminently paintable. She knew her father could do a wonderful portrait of him, but she very much doubted whether he would be up for a commission.

"So you have a permanent reminder of your mother," she said with gentle compassion. "I'm so sorry for your loss. The feeling of being deprived of your mother must never go away. I'm very close to my mother. I can't imagine life without her."

"Then you're blessed," he said, looking across the small circular table and right into her eyes.

Really looking—as though she was in some way important to him or his agenda.

"And you have both your parents," he continued. "My father died a few years back."

Just as Mark had said. She'd concluded Blaine Kilcullen was a man of iron control, but a flash of pain crossed his chiselled features.

"Dad remarried, according to Adeline, to give me a stepmother." He didn't tell her Adeline had actually said a ready-made nanny. Everyone in the family knew his father's marriage to Hilary had been one of convenience, although Hilary, daughter of a pastoralist friend of the family, had long idolized Desmond Kilcullen from afar.

"Mark never made it clear you and he were half brothers. He always talked about you as though you were—well…full brothers."

"Did he?" He took care to keep his tone even. He could well imagine what Mark had told them all, the damage Mark had done. Not only to him, but to the rest of the family. Mark had near destroyed himself with bitterness and resentment. "Mark was still engaged to a very nice young woman when he took off without a word to anyone," he said, just to put part of the record straight. "He jumped on a freight plane that had flown machinery into the station, as it happened. From the look on your face you didn't know about that either."

"Remember, please," she said again, "I'm Amanda's cousin." She needed to explain her lack of knowledge.

"But you are close?" He resumed his piercing silver-grey scrutiny.

She hoped she didn't flush. She and Amanda had co-existed rather than ever growing close as she had hoped. The closeness simply hadn't happened. "Amanda's parents were killed when she was five. Her parents were returning from a long trip and her father apparently fell asleep at the wheel. *My* mother and father opened up their home and their hearts to Amanda. Amanda, my brother Emile and I all grew up together. He's a highly gifted architect and interior designer."

"So the artistic gift runs in the family?" he said. "May I ask what *you* do?"

He actually sounded interested. "I manage one of my father's galleries, and I paint myself. As you say, it's in the blood."

"Do you show your work?"

She gave him a sparkling glance. He knew the sparkle was unconscious, but a man could find it powerfully seductive. "I've had four showings up to date. Each time they become more successful. I specialize in landscapes, the occasional still-life. My father's speciality is portraiture, though he can paint anything. Many of his subjects have been very important people, and of course very beautiful women. My father worships a woman's beauty. I'm not in his league—" she smiled "—but Lucien is wonderfully supportive. Which is not to say he isn't highly critical when he feels the need. My brother loves Dad but he took off to New York to make his own way in the world. When Emile is home it's like being around twins—Dad and Emile are so much alike." She changed the subject, although she could see his interest was unfeigned. "Did you know Amanda and Mark actually met in Paris, not here in Vancouver?"

He gritted fine white teeth. "Sienna, it was Mark's plan to vanish into thin air. At that time he was a very disturbed young man." No need to add that he'd had chips as big as desert boulders on both shoulders.

"You don't want me to press you about Mark?" At her question he gave her a searching look. It was as though he wanted to know everything that went on inside her.

"I think I have summed it up," he said in a clipped voice.

"Perhaps you should know what he thought of *you*?" Unforgivably, she was returning his brusqueness.

"Not right now," he said. "Mark was family. His death matters."

He had turned the tables on her. She felt

ashamed of herself. "Of course it matters. Please forgive me. I only thought it would explain so much about Amanda if I could tell you—"

"That Mark hated me?" His black brows rose. "Sienna, I *know*. It was a very bad case of sibling rivalry. We all live in isolation on a vast Outback station, yet Mark and I never really connected. We never did things together. It's hard to explain."

Not to me, she thought. It was almost exactly her experience with Amanda.

"I was my father's heir. His firstborn. Mark grew up knowing I was the one who would inherit Katajannga. That's the name of our cattle station. Not that he had any interest in being or becoming a cattle man."

Her interest had soared. "That's the name of your station? Katajannga? How extraordinary Mark never mentioned that."

"Mark kept a lot of things locked up," he said sombrely. "There's a long story attached to the name. It more or less means 'revelation', or sometimes 'many lagoons' when translated from the aboriginal. One can understand why. After good rains the desert is indeed a revelation."

Her beautiful eyes, fixed on his, revealed her fascination. "I'm here to listen."

"When Mark's wife is not?"

She sat back abruptly, trying to interpret the question. "You said that as though you're trying to catch me out?"

"Did I?" He didn't back down.

"I can't be held responsible for Amanda, you know."

"Of course not. But I have the feeling you're covering for her now."

She released the breath she'd been holding. "Amanda just can't deal with this now, Mr Kilcullen. Surely you understand?"

Heightened feelings were contagious. "How well did you know Mark?"

A flash of temper put fire in her deep golden eyes. "As well as anyone knew him."

"An odd answer, surely? Or do you mean his wife aside?"

"Please don't hassle me, Mr Kilcullen," she said, sitting straighter.

"God forbid!" A smile tugged at his mouth. "And I insist you call me Blaine. After all, you invited me to call you Sienna. I'm not a monster, you know."

"Aren't you?" Mark had really hated him.

He read her mind. "Probably Mark's *exact* word. Monster. Should I be offended?"

Colour rose beneath her lovely creamy skin. "I'm just seeking the truth."

He lifted his brandy balloon, took a mouthful, savouring it before responding. "Sienna, Mark may have seen me that way," he said tersely, "but I'd like *you* to keep an open mind. You won't find anyone from where I come from to hang a label like that on me. In fact anyone who tried to would be in for a hard time. My father was a greatly respected man. 'The Kilcullen' he was always called, as his father, his grandfather and great-grandfather before him. He was my role model. I could never let him down."

Had that made less room for Mark? "I would think your father regarded you as the perfect son. Would you say Mark let him down?" Mark, being Mark, would have done just that. He had certainly let his wife down. "You would have been your father's golden boy." She pinned that silvery gaze, knowing she was acting out of character but she couldn't seem to help herself. He was a very provoking man.

"Wrong colouring, surely?" His handsome face relaxed into another half-smile. "Golden boy fitted Mark much better."

He should smile more often, she thought. It was a stunning illumination. "This *has* to be confusing." She focused on a beautiful arrangement of flowers nearby. They would all have to rethink everything damning Mark had uttered about his family.

"It will be confusing when one feels compelled to change one's opinion. I have a fair idea of what Mark told his wife. And *you*. He would have told you, of course."

She took a full minute to answer, not ready for this. "Why 'of course'? What could you be implying?" She hoped to God she hadn't flushed. She wanted to keep her explosive memories of Mark private—especially from his half-brother.

"Let's call it a desire to know what happened to my half-brother. As far as my family is aware you were the one person outside Amanda that Mark didn't hate or resent in some way. Mark fed on resentment."

That was her own judgement, yet she felt as if she was being dragged into a deep, murky pond. "Let's get this straight," she said. "When exactly did Mark talk about me? More to the point, *why*? I didn't see Mark all that much." *Made sure I didn't.*

He tossed back the remainder of his cognac. "Don't let me upset you, Sienna. None of this is easy. I only mean Mark obviously thought very highly of you. He wrote about you to his mother. That's if you were Amanda's bridesmaid and her best friend?"

"I *was* my cousin's bridesmaid." She frowned in perplexity.

"As I thought. Only Mark failed to mention you and Amanda were related. Knowing Mark, I would say it was a deliberate oversight. Hilary insisted on showing me his letter, although I didn't particularly want to read it or even know what Mark had to say at the time."

"Well, you could tell me *now*." She settled her gaze on him. "The notion that he bothered to write about me at all doesn't make a whole lot of sense. What *did* he say? Mark had good-looks, and an easy charm when the mood took him. That would be no surprise to you. But to be painfully honest we didn't get to be friends."

"Except Mark didn't see it that way." His shapely hand gently rocked his empty brandy balloon. "Not so surprising when one thinks about it. Mark believed what he wanted to believe."

"Which, in my case, was what?" she asked, with more than a touch of asperity.

"Well, you *are* a very beautiful woman. And you seem to have been important to Mark."

She gave an exasperated groan. "If I *was*, he didn't share that with me." She had no alternative but to lie. "What has that got to do with anything anyway?" she asked. "Mark fell in love with *Amanda*. Mark married *Amanda*. End of story."

"Only you know the story, Sienna. We don't. But I'm more than prepared to listen to anything you want to tell me. The marriage was happy?"

"Why wouldn't it have been?" she parried. She wasn't about to tell him there had been lots of crises, rows, Amanda in floods of tears. What good would it do?

He studied her. "The simple answer. I *knew* Mark."

She had known him too. "It was happy enough,"

she answered, caught up in a swirl of emotion. Even the air seemed charged.

"You were there when he had his fatal accident?"

Memory swept over her. She lowered her head, unaware the light was bouncing off her rose-gold hair. "Yes. Amanda had invited me along." She had only relented and gone because Amanda had seemed desperate she join them at the ski resort. She still didn't know why Amanda had appeared so distraught. "I don't need to tell you Mark had a reckless streak. Amanda and I are experienced skiers. We've been skiing all our lives. Mark, very tragically, thought he was a lot better than he actually was. It was a terrible day. Amanda went totally to pieces."

"But *you* didn't?"

Her eyes flashed. "That sounds remarkably like an accusation of sorts." Her response was just as terse as his question. "I was deeply shocked and saddened, of course, but I was glad I was there. Amanda needed me." Amanda was one of the neediest young women in the world. But no need to tell him *that* either.

His eyes lingered on her beautiful face, now

flushed with colour. He had angered her. But it couldn't be avoided. "You do know I'm here to arrange for Mark's body to be shipped home? I also want to invite Amanda to return with me. She must want to attend Mark's funeral, surely? And she can finally meet the family. We will, of course, meet all her costs. Do you think she would do that?"

Sienna had to take time before she could answer. "Blaine," she said in a subdued voice, "Amanda is rather a fragile person."

"And you're her anchor?"

"I've always looked out for her," she admitted. "We've all deemed it important to look out for Amanda. She lost both her parents at such an early age. I must tell you she couldn't have found better foster parents than my mother and father. There were and remain kindness itself."

"I'm sure of that," he said. "Hilary said your father sounded very kind and compassionate. But you don't think Amanda will meet me, let alone come back to Australia with me?"

She stopped him by placing the tips of her fingers very briefly over his. It was a totally spontaneous action born of compassion. "I'm so sorry," she said.

Her skin was warm and as soft as silk, yet it sent tremors shooting down his spine. "I don't want to go back without her." His expression tautened. "She should *want* to attend Mark's funeral, surely? She did agree to our taking his body home. And as Mark's widow she stands to inherit money. I administer the Kilcullen Family Trust now my father has gone. I can make it easy for Amanda to access her inheritance or difficult for her to gain control of the funds. I don't think she should escape meeting her late husband's family at long last. Hilary will welcome her. So will Marcia, Mark's twin." He was far from sure in Marcia's case. Both Mark and Marcia had inherited difficult natures. Not from Hilary, herself but Hilary's family.

Mark had left them right out of the loop, Sienna inwardly lamented. "Mark never once said he had a twin. He could only be drawn on you."

Blaine shrugged an impeccably tailored shoulder. His tone was ironic. "I expect there's an avalanche of things you don't know. Do you think the trip back to Australia would be made easier if you accompanied your cousin?"

His suggestion rocked her. It also gave her a totally unprepared for thrill.

"That's if you could possibly spare the time?" he said. "I could hang on for a day or two. As an artist, I think you'll find our Channel Country has a lot to offer. At the moment it's boom time. We've had record rains over the past couple of years. The desert dunes are thickly clothed in green. There are wild flowers as far as the eye can see. Flood waters have even rolled into Lake Eyre, turning it into the fabled inland sea of pre-history. A number of Australian landscape artists have stayed with us on the station of recent times. And Hilary and Marcia love company."

"You've quite astonished me." She was unable to free herself from his gaze. It was downright mesmerizing.

"But the idea isn't entirely unacceptable to you?" Brackets framed his mouth. Amusement? Triumph? She couldn't tell. He was a man of con-tradictions.

"Perhaps…" She found herself admitting, "But you don't know me! I'm a stranger."

"Oddly enough, you don't seem like a stranger to me." The remark was delivered without his thinking, yet it had sprung from deep inside him. More than one switch had been turned on, he thought with a degree of self mockery. He had more than enough problems, yet he *wanted* this woman to come. He wanted to see her on his own land. He had never remotely expected this. being exploited, perhaps, by a beautiful woman wasn't on his agenda.

Sienna, ever perceptive, had caught the subtle nuance. The level of intensity between them had gone up several notches. She dropped her eyes, startled to discover she was powerfully attracted to Mark's 'Lucifer'. Attraction was beyond anyone's control, she excused herself. It simply *happened*. Often when one least needed it to happen.

"So many things we've lived with without knowing," she said ruefully.

"There are things that you *need* to know. Amanda, you, your family who raised her. Surely you all thought it extremely odd that Mark didn't reach out and at least invite his mother and his twin to his wedding?"

There was a fraught pause. Sienna stared back at the beautiful flower arrangement, seeking a moment of calm. "Of course we did!" Her tone showed more upset than she'd intended. "Especially in relation to his mother. We didn't know about Mark's twin. But it was Mark's decision. Amanda did everything he asked of her. She fell blindly in love with him. As you've guessed, things changed."

"And they've changed even more drastically now Mark's dead," he said, his expression sombre. "He can no longer dictate his widow's actions. She'll be given an opportunity to find out what Mark's family is really like. As you're so close, I'm hoping you'll be able to persuade her, Sienna. And there *is* the money," he added somewhat dryly. "What exactly does Amanda do? I'm assuming as she and Mark were childless she has a career?"

She could hardly say, as was actually the case, that Amanda shared Mark's aversion to work.

"Mark didn't want Amanda to take a job during their marriage. She had to be there for him at all times."

"I see." He didn't look surprised. "And what did Mark work at?"

She took a deep breath. "This and that," she said evasively. "He found jobs easily in the hospitality industry. That seemed to suit him. What does it matter now? Mark always had money. We assumed he had private means."

"He had a bottomless well," Blaine announced in a very crisp voice. "His mother. The mother he didn't want to see. But he was quite happy to take her money. As far as I'm aware—I could be wrong—my stepmother kept in fairly constant touch with Mark."

"She would have wanted to, as his mother. The whole situation defies belief! But it's really none of my business."

He made a jeering sound. "Oh, I think it is. You're *here*, aren't you? You're standing in for your cousin. You obviously protect her. If Amanda needs to be talked into coming back with me, I would say you're the one to do it. You'd be very welcome to come too—as in Amanda's case, with all expenses paid. You would be doing us a huge favour. The past has to be washed clean. All the things that were kept secret brought out into the open. Much healthier that way."

"I can't work miracles," she said, averting her head.

Her profile was exquisite. She was a very beautiful woman. But there was nothing threatening in her style of beauty. She had been born with natural charm. "So much for the migraine!" he returned, very coolly.

She felt hot blood flushing through her. "She's in *pain*," she burst out. "She did love him, you know."

He responded bluntly. "Only—very sadly for Amanda—he fell out of love with *her*. If indeed he was ever in love with her. Mark lost interest in most things very fast. He left behind him a young woman who believed he loved her. They were engaged to be married. Mark's mother was convinced Joanne would be the ideal young woman to lend Mark much needed strength and support. He rejected it from the rest of us. Joanne is a fine young woman. Our pioneering families have always been close."

"So chances are Joanne will hate Amanda? If she comes to the funeral they will come face to face."

"Time has passed, Sienna," he offered, with a spread of his elegant tanned hands.

"Not enough time, I would think. A wounded heart can't heal overnight."

He studied her wonderfully expressive face. "You sound very sure. Has anyone wounded *your* heart?"

"Of course. A little," she said lightly. "I'm twenty-six, but no real heartache to speak of. I'm prepared to wait for the right man to come along. And what about you, Blaine? You're good with the questions. What about a few answers? You're not married?"

"Finding the right wife would be a whole lot easier if I had more time," he said. "If you visit the station you'll realize I have a big job on my hands. We all thought my father was going to live for ever. He was such a force! So strong and powerful. It was unbearable to see him struck down. It changed my life. It changed all our lives."

"Can you speak about it?" she asked gently.

"Mark never did?"

His light eyes really did *glitter*. He must have inherited those remarkable eyes from someone. Father? Or the mother who had died so young? "Not beyond the fact your father had died. He wasn't forthcoming about *how*."

"I imagine not," he said grimly. "It was Mark who found him lying crippled and unconscious out in the desert." The vibrancy of his voice had been damped right down. "It was the big muster. Somehow Dad and Mark became separated from our group. We all thought Mark had packed it in. He had a habit of doing that. Dad had probably gone after him, to pull him back into line. Anyway, Mark galloped frenziedly into the lignum swamps, where we were flushing out unbranded cattle, yelling near incoherently that Dad was dead. Duchess, my father's very special mare, had thrown him and then trampled him into the ground. Mark had taken his rifle and shot the mare in a fit of grief and rage."

He remembered how wave after wave of waterfowl had risen in fright and outrage at the racket Mark was making. How every last man had stood in a devastated gut-wrenching silence at the drastic news. Everyone had confidently expected Desmond Kilcullen to live for many more years, liked and respected by the entire Outback community.

His pain was so palpable it stabbed at her. "How horrendous!" Sienna was about able to visualize the tragic scene.

"Horrendous, indeed." He underscored her comment. "I damn nearly dropped dead myself from shock. According to Mark, Duchess had kicked Dad in the head. Accidents always will happen around horses, but my father was a consummate horseman. And Duchess was a wonderful one man horse. Something unexplained must have freaked the mare out. If terrified she would have reacted convulsively, throwing my unprepared father. Mark shot the mare on the spot. Dad spent the few remaining years of his life in a wheelchair, his memory of that terrible day blasted from his mind." He didn't add that any semblance of family life had been shattered.

Sienna sat horrified. "I'm so sorry Mark mistook your father's condition."

"I don't know how, but he did," he told her bleakly. "He was in a massive panic."

"It's such a terrible story." She considered a moment. "Do you think it could have caused Mark's subsequent behaviour? Could he have felt some measure of guilt? I mean in the sense that he was the one to find your father. He had to shoot the mare. Was the mare a very temperamental animal?"

The handsome features visibly tightened, highlighting his fine bone structure. "Duchess was a very special horse, so of course she was a spirited animal. Something must have badly spooked her, as I've said. Mark was nearly off his head at the time. No one could get much sense out of him—*especially* me. He acted like I was accusing him of something. Dad could recall nothing of that day, although much of his past memory came back over time."

"So you never could piece the exact sequence of events together?"

"No." His expression grew darker.

Two tragic accidents that had claimed father and now son. "When did Mark abandon his family and fiancée, exactly?"

"Far too soon." He didn't tell her Mark had shied clear of visiting their father in hospital.

Mark had been long gone before their father's second unsuccessful back operation.

"Mark must have been crushed, given what had happened," she offered, as some sort of mitigating circumstance.

"It was my father who was crushed."

"Sorry, sorry—wrong word," she apologized. "But Mark could well have felt guilt. Would *you* have shot the mare?' She waited, wanting his answer.

"No." His reply was emphatic. "My father wouldn't have wanted it. I have to see it this way: something spooked the mare. An encounter with a camel in heat is a possible explanation. They can be ferocious. Male camels come on heat, not the female. They can't be avoided. They're part of the Outback now. They were brought in by Afghan traders in the early days of settlement. They thrived."

"So it could have been a rogue camel, then?" she asked.

He shot her a searching look. "There was any number in the area. But we were all well aware of that. Dad had handled plenty of rogue camels. I have myself. One doesn't waste a moment getting away. Or, if forced to, one takes the camel out. They come at full charge."

"So there remains a question hanging over that dreadful day?"

He took his time to answer. "A question that will never be answered, Sienna. Dad is dead. A disaster that fell like an impenetrable fog over our lives. It has never lifted. Now Mark is dead too."

"How much sadder could that be?" She bowed her head.

"Sienna, I must appeal to you to speak to Amanda on my behalf." He spoke more urgently. "This is no time for inaction. Mark was her husband. I want her to come back to Australia with me. She won't be alone in her grief. Hilary loved her son. She missed him every single day he was gone."

"Of course she would, as his mother." She well understood the strength of the bond. She was very close to her own mother. "And he did write to her, if only to inform her of his marriage. But his twin? Marcia? You seem to have avoided mentioning her much?"

She was proving very insightful. "Strangely enough, the twins didn't get on all that well. They could be antagonistic, although they understood one another completely. Marcia isn't feeling her twin's loss like their mother. Which is not to reduce the close bond entirely—Marcia is deeply distressed. I'm afraid Mark's behaviour put us all off side. Marcia and Joanne remain good friends. Marcia felt Joanne's pain of betrayal. If Mark thought he was abandoned it wasn't true. Leaving was Mark's choice. It was his family and his fiancée who felt abandoned. I think it's time now to bring closure. If Amanda can't do it on her own, you're the one who can help her."

Some strong communication was passing between them. She couldn't begin to speculate on what it was. All she knew for sure was that he had made it sound as if her very destiny hinged on her going to Australia.

CHAPTER TWO

SIENNA was hardly inside the door of her apartment when the phone rang. She didn't hurry to answer it. It could only be Amanda, wanting a second-by-second account of how the evening had gone. That was Amanda! It was well after midnight. But time—everyone else's time—meant nothing to her cousin. Maybe some time soon the family could start treating Amanda like a woman instead of an ever needful little girl. It was a role Amanda had settled into as the best and easiest way to get her through life. Now her husband's tragic end. No one could have foreseen that. Amanda needed support. It always had been Sienna's job to prop her cousin up. At such a time as now it would be cruel not to.

"Hell, Sienna, have you only just got home?" A slurred and highly irritable voice greeted her.

Amanda's modus operandi was to put her on

the back foot. Sienna drew a calming breath. "Hi, Mandy. Calm down, now. I fully intended to ring you first thing in the morning. Can't it wait? It's well after midnight." Blaine Kilcullen had insisted on seeing her home. They'd had to wait for a cab. Despite all her earlier misgivings time had flown. One could even say *on wings*. The man was so charismatic a woman might well need to build protective walls.

"No, it can't!" Amanda retorted. "I'm ill with grief."

Of course she was. Sienna softened her stand. "I'm sorry, Mandy. I truly am. But drink won't help."

"Always the role model!" Amanda warbled. "As if that's all there is to life—being a role model. My wonderful, clever, oh-so-beautiful cousin." A pause while she took another gulp of whatever drink was to hand. Vodka, most likely. Amanda had started bending her elbow not all that long into her marriage. Now it was getting out of hand. "Tried to take him off me, didn't you?" Amanda was back to her sickening accusations. "It wasn't me who made my dear husband's hormones soar.

It was *you*—and I was powerless to do anything about it."

It had taken Sienna many years to recognize Amanda's jealousies and deep resentments. People had pointed it out to her over the years but she had chosen not to listen. "Amanda, please stop this" She tried to ignore the sick lurch in her stomach. "We've been over it too many times. I was *not* attracted to Mark. Mark was *your* husband. If he'd been the sexiest man in the world—which he wasn't—he'd have been totally off-limits. I refuse to be drawn into any more discussions on the subject, much as you're compelled to bring it up."

Amanda must have made a wild sweep with her hand, because Sienna could hear glass breaking. Probably the glass she'd been drinking out of.

"Aren't you forgetting I discovered the two of you together?" Amanda raged on, in that upsettingly slurred voice.

"Face it, Amanda. You *know* the truth." Yet irrational guilt settled hard and heavy on Sienna's shoulders. Her conscience couldn't have been clearer in regard to that appalling evening. Still she felt a measure of guilt for the pain that had been caused to her all too vulnerable cousin.

"He *loved* you—don't you realize that?"

Sienna held the phone away from her ear. "What Mark loved was creating great disharmony. You're upsetting us both with this talk, Amanda. My sole loyalty is to you. Look, I can't talk to you while you're in this mood. I'm going to hang up now. Get some sleep. I promise I'll ring you in the morning."

"You'd better!"

The force of the threat stopped Sienna in her tracks. "Don't make me withdraw my support, Amanda," she said quietly. "And by the way, Mark's *half*-brother—he didn't tell us that, did he?—is nothing like Mark tried so hard to present him. He's a very impressive man." The polar opposite of everything that had been Mark.

"Such camaraderie in a few short hours!" Amanda hooted. "Just tell me this. Is there any money? Did he look like he's got pots of money? God knows, Mark left me with nothing."

But Amanda had always had a safety net in the family. They would have been expected to pick up the shambles Amanda had made of her life. But now there was Kilcullen money. "To be fair to Mark, he did keep you both in some style. Apparently his mother proved to be a bottomless well when he needed topping up. She must have done it pretty regularly. And just look how he treated her! I'll tell you another thing, so you can sleep on it. Blaine—"

"Blaine?"

Sienna moved the phone away from her ear again. "I can hardly refer to him as Mr Kilcullen," she said, suddenly sick to death of her cousin. "Your late husband's *half*-brother very much wants you to accompany him back to Australia. He's assured me you will be welcomed. Mark has a twin, by the way, name of Marcia. Apparently they weren't all that close—unlike most twins." Now definitely wasn't the time for Amanda to learn about the scorned fiancée.

"Mark wouldn't have deliberately lied to me," Amanda asserted in a thick voice, when her normal tones were soft and breathy.

"Mark had a twin, Amanda," Sienna said. "The truth was an alien concept to him. He lied to us all the time. He kept his true self and his true life well under wraps. Probably he was laughing at us. He had a cruel streak."

"He was a *fabulous* husband."

Clearly Amanda was in denial. "Mandy, you contradict yourself all the time. Why were you always so desperate for me to join you and Mark? You never did explain. Was the marriage all but over? Was that what it was all about, Mandy? Do you *ever* come clean?"

Silence for a moment, then Amanda's harsh reaction. "I need you to understand something, Sienna. If my marriage was over, it was because of *you*. You had to take the one thing I had."

Sienna was too appalled to continue. Drink turned some people happy. It turned others abusive. "I'm hanging up now, Amanda," she said, thinking things would never get better. Amanda would most probably worsen. "You've been drinking. You don't know what you're saying. You're exhausting my good will. In case you're thinking of ringing back, I'm taking the phone off the hook."

"Do it. Go on—do it!" Amanda urged, her voice rising to a crescendo.

Sienna did, wrapping her arms around herself.

There were only two ways to deal with Amanda. Put up with her, or remove her from her life. After all these years since decided she could never do that. Maybe a good man would come along to take care of her cousin.

Sienna was upstairs, talking to valued client and family friend Nadine Duval, when Amanda walked through the front door of the gallery.

"Sienna, where are you?"

Her voice was pitched so high and loud it was startling. It echoed right through the large open space, its white walls hung with stunning paintings from her father's last sell-out showing. In the last fifteen years Lucien Fleury had moved on to international eminence with numerous critically acclaimed exhibitions. Sienna was enormously proud of him. He in turn was enormously proud of both his children. Both had been hailed as major talents.

"In the genes, Sienna, my darling."

Of course he took the credit.

Nadine Duval, an extremely rich woman, who had paid a fortune for arguably her father's finest canvas in the showing, gave her an understanding little smile. "That will be Amanda, poor girl. We all feel so sorry for her, but I just bet she's giving you a bad time. You have to get free of her, Sienna," Nadine warned, not for the first time. "The girl is trouble."

"Well she's suffering now," Sienna explained, beginning to walk Nadine down the spiral staircase.

"Of course she is." Nadine's response was vaguely ironic.

"I'll have the painting delivered this afternoon," Sienna promised, when they arrived at the bottom.

Nadine reached for her hand. "Thank you, my dear. Tell Lucien I want to see him. Maybe lunch?"

"Will do."

They exchanged kisses.

Amanda looked far more fragile than the strength of her voice had suggested. Indeed she looked waif-like. She had lost weight when she couldn't afford to do so. Her skin, her best feature, was so pale it was almost translucent. She had violet half-moons beneath her eyes, and the silky curls of her pretty blonde hair had lost their lustre and bounce.

"I really don't like that woman," she growled.

It was a mercy Nadine had gone through the door to her waiting limousine.

"Your loss, Mandy. Nadine has so much character."

"And of course she loves you too." Amanda was looking hung over, and haggard for her years.

"I hope you haven't come here to make a scene, Amanda." Sienna was worried that just might happen. It was fortunate that, with the exhibition over, all that remained was for her to have the paintings delivered to their clients. That meant fewer visitors to the gallery.

"Nothing matters. Nothing matters any more," Amanda said, face and voice full of woe.

Sienna's tender heart smote her. "Come through to the office. Would you like a cup of coffee? You don't look good, Amanda. I know this is a terrible time, but you have to take care of yourself."

"*Why*, exactly?" Amanda asked bitterly, sinking her fingers into the skin of her face and dragging her eyes down. "I know I look awful. No need to rub it in."

"I hope I wasn't doing that. I care about you, Mandy. We'll *all* help you work through your grief."

"Who's *all*?" Amanda shot back, as if she had been fiercely rejected all her life instead of cosseted. "I hardly see Aunty Francine."

"She works, Amanda, as well you know. But she does ring you often," Sienna reminded her. Like the rest of them, Francine had tried hard to take to Mark, but found she couldn't. Consequently, as often happened, it had put distance between them all. "The family are busy people with busy lives, Amanda. But we're all there for you when we're needed. Come and sit down," she urged, putting out a sheltering arm. "I have things to tell you."

Once seated in the office, Amanda began to gnaw on her nails. "It's taking all my energy just to stay alive."

Sienna risked another caution. "You have to stop drinking, Mandy."

"I need something to get me through,' Amanda maintained doggedly.

Sienna made coffee from her excellent little machine, adding cream from the refrigerator and two teaspoons of sugar. "I have some cookies if you want them?"

Amanda laughed shortly. "I can't get a thing down my throat.' She looked up, her blue eyes moist, her expression wretched. "What am I going to do, Sienna? What sort of a job am I going to get? I was never a good student. Not like *you*. I didn't make university. Not only did you get all the looks, you got all the brains and a gift for painting."

"From Lucien," Sienna acknowledged, taking a seat behind her mahogany desk. "Drink up, and I'll tell you what Blaine Kilcullen had to say."

"It had better be good," Amanda warned. "What a shocking lot those people are. How cruel they were to Mark."

"There are two sides to a story, Amanda," Sienna said quietly, not wanting to provoke her cousin. "Mark did his level best to put us off his family."

"He had good reasons." Wrath registered on Amanda's white face.

Mark had seen himself as a victim. It struck Sienna that was the way Amanda saw herself too. It showed a link between them. All the bad things that happened in life were never *their* fault. The fault lay with others. Both had dark places.

"Oh, my God, Sienna!" Amanda cried, when Sienna had finished outlining Blaine Kilcullen's proposal. "There's money!" She gave a great cry of relief.

"The Kilcullens aren't going to see you in financial trouble, Mandy." So much for the Fleury family's generosity! She recalled one of her father's recent comments.

"She's not you, my darling, frail little creature that she is!"

"I don't know exactly how much, but I'd say a substantial sum. Blaine administers a family trust. After meeting him, I have to say I don't see him as the ogre Mark made him out."

"Lucifer, don't you mean?" Amanda cried, not about to put all the things Mark had said behind her. "The fallen angel. Does he look like Mark?" she asked. "I don't know if that would make me feel better or worse."

Sienna shook her head. "You wouldn't spot the relationship, but he is a half-brother. He's dark, with the most remarkable light eyes."

"So he got to you, did he?" Amanda shot her a

look full of malice. "Did you get to *him*? That's your speciality, isn't it? Getting to guys, fascinating them."

Sienna threw up her hands in defeat. "You'd use a sledgehammer on me if you could, Amanda. At the same time you *use* me—and I allow it. Not for much longer."

"Okay, I'm sorry." Amanda backed off when she saw her cousin really meant it. "I'm just so sick with worry and grief." Tears oozed out of her eyes.

"I understand that." Sienna relented, as usual, although she knew Amanda could turn tears on and off at will. "Would you consider going to Australia?"

Amanda quelled the tears. "I could never go without you," she declared flatly. "You've looked after me since we were kids. I need you, Sienna. Only you could get me through."

Sienna felt a rush of warmth. Not at what Amanda had said, but at the involuntary exhilaration she felt at the idea of going to Australia. "Time is of the essence," she said. "He has to fly back home. He has a vast cattle station to look after, big responsibilities."

"And he doesn't feel *guilty*?" Amanda with one of her lightning changes of mood, banged the table. "He got through to *you*, all right, but *I'm* a different story. I'm Mark's widow. Mark told me everything, how his brother ruined his life."

"Half-brother," Sienna corrected. "There was a tremendous amount of conflict in Mark."

"It's not the first time you've tried to malign Mark." Amanda made it perfectly plain Sienna's observations were unwelcome.

"I'm not maligning him, Mandy. I'm trying to point out some reason for all the discrepancies. He never told you about his twin. He never told you he was getting money from his mother. Mark's account of his past life was all we had to go on up until I met Blaine Kilcullen. If you agree to meet him you can make up your own mind. It's your decision, Amanda."

"Why can't he just give me the money?" Amanda suggested, looking hopeful. "I'm entitled to it."

"And Mark's mother and sister are entitled to meet you," Sienna said, more sharply than she had intended. "You gave permission for his family to ship his body home. Surely you can find it within yourself to meet them and attend Mark's funeral?"

"I don't *want* to." Amanda started to work herself into one of her rages. "I hate them. I hate Mark for the things he did to me."

"*What* things?" Sienna trapped her cousin's darting eyes. "What is it you're keeping to yourself? The reason you wanted me at the ski resort? I thought it very odd, considering the number of times you'd warned me off."

"I wanted to have it out with him. I wanted you there."

Sienna released a long breath. "You're lying. You've been lying all your life—" She broke off abruptly. "I'm sorry. I shouldn't have said that. But you're not telling me the truth."

"The truth will go with Mark into his grave," Amanda said bleakly. "When does this man want me to meet him? I can't do it today. I have to have my hair done."

"Does this mean you *will* go, Amanda? If you want me to go with you I have to make urgent arrangements."

"Really? The only thing you need to do is tell your father," Amanda sneered. "He'll find a stand-in. Lucien *adores* his beautiful Sienna, with the marvellous hair and the matching amber eyes. He's told everybody *you* are his favourite model."

"After my *mother*," Sienna contradicted. "I am no way as beautiful as my mother."

"Who would believe you?" Amanda's voice was brittle enough to break.

Sienna sat back, feeling defeated. "Amanda, we've all done our best for you, yet you keep slamming us with insults even when you put your hands out for money. I do care for you, Amanda. But I need your definite answer now."

Tears sprang into Amanda's eyes. "Do you have to be so dictatorial? You have to give me time."

Sienna shook her head. "There's little time available." She rose as she heard the buzzer signalling someone had entered the gallery.

"If that's another client get rid of them," Amanda's tears miraculously dried up.

"It might take a minute or two. Stay here."

She walked out into the main room, startled to see the visitor to the gallery was none other than Blaine Kilcullen, cattle baron. She couldn't help noting he looked marvelous: handsome, powerful, successful—someone very special. He had been studying her father's remaining paintings—many had already been delivered—and now he turned his raven head to her. "Good afternoon, Sienna."

She felt heat sweep her body when all he had done was say good afternoon.

"I thought, while I could, I'd take a look at the gallery," he explained. "Your father has an international reputation, I understand? Looking at these paintings, I can see why. This portrait of you is stunning!"

He stood directly in front of the bravura portrait—a homage to a young woman's beauty. The canvas shimmered with light. The treatment of her flesh was so good he had an urge to stroke, to check if the bloom was real. Her long hair had unfurled all around her face and cascaded down her back. The *exactness* of the colour of hair and skin was amazing. She was posed tucked into a roomy gilded armchair, clearly French, so the lovely pattern of the silk upholstery added to the arrangement. One bare arm hung over the side, her fingers curving over the gilded wood. She was wearing a long strapless dress in palest gold. Citrine and diamond drop earrings picked up the colour, as did a matching citrine and diamond pendant enclosed in swirls of gold that drew his eye to the high, youthful curves of her breasts.

"It's not for sale," she explained. "My father won't part with it."

"I don't blame him."

She felt the flush that came to her cheeks. "He looks on it as a lucky talisman for opening nights. I was about to turn twenty-one when he painted it. The earrings and pendant were my parents' gift to me. I should tell you my mother is the real beauty in the family. I thought the portrait was going to be a present for me, but he kept it himself." She laughed at the memory. "One never knows what to expect with Lucien. It flatters me."

In no way was she fishing for compliments, he thought. She genuinely believed the portrait *did* flatter her. "I disagree." He remained in place, studying the luminous canvas. "Have you had an opportunity to speak to Amanda?"

"I have, actually."

"And?" He turned to her with his diamond-sharp gaze.

It was at that precise moment Amanda chose to appear—an actress entering from the wings to take centre stage. In the interim she had somehow managed to transform herself. From looking like a rag doll she was now looking almost perky. She had fluffed up her blonde curls and applied some make-up to good effect. She might even have used eyedrops because her blue eyes were wide and strangely bright.

"Blaine, at long last we meet!" She came forward with not one but two arms outstretched.

Award-winning material, Sienna thought. Not that she hadn't seen such transformations in the past.

Blaine Kilcullen towered over the petite Amanda. "Amanda." He took one of her hands and held it in his. "My family is hoping you will come back to Australia with me," he said. "We have a real bond through Mark."

"Of course we do!" Amanda said with a little emotional heave of her chest. "Sienna has been begging me to come too."

"I couldn't be more pleased if you would," he replied.

Having had the benefit of hearing the various nuances he employed in his voice, Sienna thought there was a possibility he wasn't being taken in by Amanda.

"That just leaves us to decide which day it will be," he said.

Amanda laughed gently. "I can't pack up just like that, Blaine!"

"No need to go to a great deal of trouble," he assured her. "Anything you need we can get for you at home. Just name it and it will be flown in."

Amanda allowed herself a poignant smile. "You're so kind. And I will have Sienna to help me. Would Wednesday suit?"

He inclined his handsome dark head. "Now that we have the day I can make all necessary arrangements." He turned to the silent Sienna. "I hope that suits you too, Sienna?"

"It's okay—don't worry," Amanda broke in. "Sienna can do whatever she likes."

"That isn't true, Amanda." Sienna couldn't help a note of reproof.

Amanda actually giggled, as if Sienna had told a fib. "It is so."

Sienna dropped a warning hand on her cousin's arm. Wasn't she supposed to be a grief-stricken widow? The trouble was Amanda was a dizzying combination of behaviours. "Just tell us what you want us to do, Blaine." She knew she spoke a little stiffly.

He quickly scanned her face. "I'll give you a ring the moment I've got everything worked out."

"We should have been good friends long ago," Amanda burst out, sounding as if she wanted to weep. "I'm so sorry about that." Her voice caught in her throat.

"We'll have time to make up for it, Amanda," the cattle baron assured her.

Sienna thought it came out a mite too suave. But she could have been wrong.

"I'll let my stepmother know immediately. She'll be greatly heartened to know you'll be coming back with me."

"Anything to soften the blow," said Amanda, fully prepared to go with the flow.

A short time later Kilcullen took his leave.

"What a hunk!" Amanda crowed. She sped back into the office, dropping into her chair. "Be still my heart! I thought Mark was good-looking, but this guy! He's a real heart-throb!"

"Who, pray, could deny it?" Sienna only half joked. Should Amanda be so focused on another man at her time of bereavement? From being prostrate with grief Amanda was now acting as if she was on the brink of an adventure. But then Amanda was prone to see-sawing emotions.

"Well, he's a lot nicer than I expected, thank you very much," Amanda said tartly. "Course, I don't know him."

"And he doesn't know *you*, Amanda. That was a great act you put on."

Amanda glared at her cousin. "Why do you always have to think the worst of me?"

"Maybe it's safer than thinking the best," Sienna offered wryly. "Do you want me to run through some of your stunts from the past?" Amanda had tried hard to break up a few of her relationships—girl friends, boyfriends—utilizing outright lies.

"You never fail to remind me," Amanda hit back with disdain. "That's the trouble with you, Sienna. You think all the good things in life should be dished up to you on a silver platter. You've had a charmed life. You don't know what it's like to feel insecure, unloved, distrusted by the people around you. You wouldn't even let me settle into my marriage."

Sienna felt a powerful wash of anger, yet she

made a superhuman effort to keep calmly afloat. "Maybe it's high time for you to consider whether it's *you* who can't relate to *us*. It's *you* who doesn't see things straight. But you've told Blaine Kilcullen you'll return to Australia with him. You've made the right decision. Indeed the only decision. You are Mark's widow. You married him. Now, very tragically, you have to bury him. That's what widows do. I'm convinced the Kilcullen family will offer you every support. And there is the *money*. As for me? I think I've run out of patience. I'm your contemporary, Amanda, not your long-suffering aunt. I'm tired of you taking out your anger and frustrations on me. You'll have to go without me."

She would make a call to Blaine Kilcullen's hotel.

Amanda jumped up like a desperately panicked woman. "No, no—you can't possibly shut me out. What would I ever do without you? You can handle people. I can't. I need someone to act as a barrier between me and these people. They'll be judging me, whatever you say. I loved Mark, but he turned out to be a real bastard. Our marriage would never have lasted. He only married me to be closer to *you*. He told me." She rounded the desk, shoving her small face into Sienna's.

Sienna pushed away in disgust.

"If you won't come with me I can't go through with it. I can't believe you'd desert me at such a terrible time.'

"And it *is* a terrible time. I accept that," Sienna returned quietly. "But it all comes down to whether I can tolerate your attacks on me."

"I don't *mean* it," Amanda cried.

Sienna closed her eyes for a moment. "You do mean it, and you enjoy it in a weird kind of way. The attacks in front of me and behind my back didn't start with Mark, either. I've only ever wanted one thing, Amanda. That was to be your *friend*. But you wouldn't let us connect. I know we have very different personalities, but you have to admit I've always been there for you."

"Of course you have!" Amanda put her hands to her aching head. "I should have died with my parents."

Sienna was overcome by remorse. "Don't say that!"

"I've been injured all the same. You don't understand. You never will. All the good fairies attended your birth. They never came to mine." She began dragging in her breath.

It was an old trick. "Relax," Sienna murmured soothingly. "You're so young. You have a lifetime ahead of you. You're very pretty and you have the brains to acquire more skills. I'll help you."

Amanda's expression sharpened. "Only I won't *want* any extra skills if I'm about to come into pots of money.'

"Oh, Amanda!" Sienna cringed.

"Blaine is much taller than Mark, isn't he?" Amanda disregarded her. "Broader in the shoulders, very handsome, and seriously sexy. A woman would feel secure with a man like that. I never thought I would say this, but I could take to Blaine. He's not married, is he?" She shot Sienna a swift glance.

Sienna just stared back. Amanda wasn't going to develop a *thing* about Blaine Kilcullen, was she? Bury one husband, plan the next? "It doesn't mean he hasn't got some very suitable woman in mind," she said firmly. "Don't daydream about Blaine Kilcullen, Amanda. He's off-limits."

Amanda smirked. "For *both* of us."

"Amanda, I'm taking that for granted," Sienna

replied. "I'd like you to go now. I have things I must do."

"Okay, I'm out of here." Amanda picked up her tote bag, then slung it over her shoulder. "If you're not going to come with me I'll ring Blaine and tell him I've thought it over, but I'm so upset it will be impossible for me to make the long flight."

"Suit yourself." Sienna pretended to search for some papers on her desk

Amanda's blue eyes darted back to her. "Stop kidding around. I can't go through with this without you. This is the last thing I'll ask of you, Sienna. Be with me now. I promise I'll be on my best behaviour."

"It's not looking that way now," Sienna said ruefully.

Amanda continued as if there had been no interruption. The fine skin of her face was mottled and she was waving her hands about as if she were under attack from a swarm of insects. "There's no one else I can ask." She swung back to Sienna, looking incredibly forlorn. "You're the one I always fall back on."

"At least you've noticed." Sienna decided not to push her cousin any further. "All right, Amanda.

We really can't go back on our promise," she said quietly. "But I have to warn you—if things start to go wrong between us once we're with the Kilcullen family I can and will fly back home. Is that understood?"

Amanda's small features started to glow with inner excitement. "But they won't go wrong. There are going to be big changes. I can feel it in my bones."

Sienna wisely remained silent.

CHAPTER THREE

THEY flew from Vancouver to Sydney—a nonstop fourteen-hour flight. Travelling first class made the long journey bearable, as did the fact they were flying southbound and westward. They had left a freezing Vancouver around midnight and arrived at Kingsford Smith International Airport mid-morning two days later, due to the time zone differences.

Blaine had organized an overnight stay at a city hotel, to give them some little time to adjust to the dreaded jet lag because their biological rhythms would be disrupted. Amanda, in particular, was showing many of the symptoms associated with flying across multiple time zones. She complained of a bad headache, and feelings of disorientation that she claimed were severe. Sienna had warned her against downing champagne during the long flight, but Amanda had rejected the fruit juices Sienna had accepted. Amanda was a grown woman, and she had become unusually aggressive since Mark's death. Sienna too was feeling below par, but as a frequent long-distance traveller she was able to cope better. She had far better tolerance and was physically fitter than her cousin who, for all her petite figure and feather weight, didn't much care for exercise.

Their passage through Customs was relatively smooth and easy. Blaine had a limousine waiting to take them to the hotel. Sienna felt very grateful for that. They were to leave for Brisbane the following morning. She understood that would involve a flight of just an hour. From Brisbane Blaine was to fly them in his own plane, a Beech Baron, to the Kilcullen cattle station in Channel Country. Sienna already knew that was in the far south-west of the huge state that was Queensland, with a population a bit smaller than the population of British Columbia but in double the area—so there had to be a vast uninhabited Outback.

Sienna stood with a quiet, humming excitement, trying to pacify a very sluggish and querulous Amanda.

"I told you I didn't want to come," Amanda

moaned. "It's too damned *far*!" She managed to make it sound as thought they had landed on Mars. "And the *heat*! It's bouncing off the pavements."

Sienna was mortified. Surely her cousin would be overheard? Blaine was standing with the limousine driver as he loaded their luggage into the boot. She was certain Blaine would have exceptionally good hearing as well as so piercing a regard, and would be able to suss out just about anything.

"Okay, I'm sorry,' Amanda apologized. "It's just that I feel lousy."

Sienna put her arm around her, offering support. "Hang in there, please, Mandy. I'll make you comfortable as soon as we reach the hotel."

"And we're nowhere near the Kilcullen station! I need sunglasses. The sunlight is *blinding*!"

It was, but Sienna found herself entranced by its quality. It was a very different light from back home, indeed from Europe, she thought. It had a radiance, an intense luminosity, that captured her artistic eye. The sky above them was a glorious cloudless blue with a shimmering veil of lavender. When they had left home the temperature at the airport had fallen dramatically even from the daytime thirty-four degrees. Here in Sydney, the largest and most cosmopolitan city in Australia, they had been informed by the plane's captain that the temperature was a fine twenty-four degrees Celsius. She knew enough about the differences between Fahrenheit and Celsius to realize the daytime temperature in Vancouver would be pretty well around zero. But then November was the end of spring in Australia. Blaine had warned them to expect heat and *more* heat as they moved north into Queensland. The Sunshine State, as it was called, straddled the Tropic of Capricorn.

Their drive into the city was undistinguishable from the drive into many other cities. Except for the fact that light summer clothing was the order of the day, the people along the way looked pretty much like everyday Canadians going about their business. Sienna remembered that a world-famous British journalist had once described Australians as the "Canadians of the South". She was really looking forward to catching a glimpse of the iconic Sydney Opera House and the Harbour Bridge. Sydney Harbour was said to be arguably the most magnificent harbour in the world. If only tragedy hadn't brought them Down Under she would have thought herself on the cusp of a great adventure...

It took a while to get Amanda settled in their beautiful luxury hotel. To Sienna's delight their suite commanded a superb vista that took in the Opera House, the Harbour Bridge and Sydney Harbour beyond, so they didn't actually have to go anywhere to see the Harbour. They had Blaine to thank for that. Making them comfortable was obviously his priority. She realized the hotel had to be in one of Sydney's most spectacular locations.

She later found out the historic Rocks area where they were was only minutes from the Harbour foreshore. Like her beautiful Vancouver, the city was set between the blue ocean and mountains, though she already knew the rugged Great Dividing Range that ran down the Australian East Coast in no way rivalled the height and majesty of the snow-capped peaks of the Canadian Rockies.

Amanda fell asleep as soon as her head hit the pillow. Sienna took a long, luxurious warm shower, and then dressed in sightseeing gear—

slim jeans, a white Herringbone cotton shirt, a fancy belt, and comfortable leather flats. She knew she had to pack sunglasses to protect her eyes, so she popped them into her tote bag. A yellow and white silk scarf tied back her long hair, topped off with a slouchy straw hat. She was to meet Blaine downstairs in ten minutes.

She had agreed with him that staying awake for a few hours after their long flight and walking around would speed up their adaptation to their current time zone. She had found in her many long travels that she suffered the worst degree of jet lag a couple of days *after* a long flight. In the meantime, she meant to make the best of her time in Sydney. The excitement she was feeling was overriding her tiredness.

Blaine Kilcullen was waiting for her in the lobby: tall, lean, and truly imposing, with his re-markable colouring, coal-black hair and brows, and silver-grey eyes. His attire was pretty much like hers—except he wore a blue cotton denim shirt with his jeans and was minus a hat. He did, however, have a pair of sunglasses tucked into his breast pocket.

His gaze swept over her as she moved towards him with a pleasant, expectant look. She had drawn her beautiful hair back tightly from face into a thick ponytail. No place to hide there. Her beauty was right on show: natural and classic. It occurred to him she didn't appear to give a lot of thought to her enviable looks. But then she *had* grown up with a very beautiful mother. He didn't doubt it for a moment.

"All set?' he asked.

"Looking forward to it." She could feel the warmth in her cheeks. Despite jet lag, she was feeling electric, her nerves buzzing inside. Meeting "Lucifer," she had to say, was the surprise of her life.

"Great. But I can't let you overdo it. We'll have a cup of coffee and a sandwich before we go. We can have it here in the hotel." He took her arm, leading the way.

"I have to thank you for going to so much trouble and expense to make Amanda and me comfortable," she said as she walked beside him. "The suite is superb. I never expected such views."

"You'll see a great deal more before you go home."

"You made that sound like a promise?"

"It is. I take it Amanda is safely tucked up in bed?"

She almost cringed. Amanda had made her irritations felt. In fact she had kept up her complaints all the way into the city. "Amanda's not a good traveller at the best of times," she explained.

"Not a good idea to drink alcohol on a long flight," he pointed out dryly.

"Amanda feels alcohol reduces the pressure she's under," she offered defensively.

"And…you have told her differently?"

"Of course I have. But who listens?" She looked up at him, revelling in his much superior height. She was taller than average. It felt good to look up to a man. "Besides, Amanda is a grown woman."

"Who is extremely fortunate to have you for a cousin."

"Is that a question of sorts?" She was trying to weigh up his inflection.

"A statement, surely?" he answered smoothly.

A current that wasn't really friction crackled back and forth between them. It was as if both thought it essential to maintain a certain distance. "I'm here as back-up," she said. "Have you given any thought to what it's like for Amanda, Blaine? Losing Mark the way she did."

His reply was swift. "Let's forget Amanda and Mark for an hour or two," he said. "Come and have that coffee."

He began to walk on—one of those men who moved with absolute self-assurance. Women turned to look at him. Why not? *She* was torn between admiring him and speculating on the inherent danger of getting any closer. She hurried to catch up. "Can you really compartmentalize your feelings so easily?" she asked.

He paused to look down at her with his piercing regard. "Call it an acquired skill, Sienna. I've learned to put unpleasant and downright disturbing things out of my head so I can get on with the job at hand. I've *had* to. I never expected to take over Katajangga for many more years, but it didn't turn out that way. Mark's death is a tragedy. I feel for Amanda. I feel for *you*."

"Why me?" Her brows peaked. "Look, Blaine, I have to dispel this notion you seem to have that Mark and I had some sort of rapport."

"If that's not the case, why did he speak of you

the way he did?" he countered. "Let's move on." He drew her away from the flow of hotel guests.

"Perhaps Mark found it essential to pull the wool over people's eyes," she suggested with a touch of heat. "I really don't know, and I really don't *care*."

"Okay. Don't get angry on such a balmy day. I know Mark would have tried to convince you and Amanda and all who would listen I was his enemy. *He* chose that way. Mark took off without a backward glance. The rest of us had to survive."

She made a soft sound of apology. "What say we call a time-out?"

He gave her a glimpse of his transforming smile. "Sounds like a good idea to me."

The following day Amanda's ill temper was directed entirely at Sienna. With Blaine she played the grief-stricken young widow, desperately in need of his strength and kindness. Amanda was never really honest with anyone. Another trait she had in common with Mark. It was hard to explain, but neither of them had wanted or indeed sought to connect with people—even the people closest to them. Bizarre as it seemed, Amanda had now turned her attention to Blaine. Maybe it was only until she got the money?

"Grieving doesn't pay the bills, Sienna. There are bills all over the place. Mark avoided paying them like the plague."

Amanda, truly exhausted and under the weather, slept on the flight to Brisbane. Sienna took ten-minute cat-naps. Far from feeling severe jet lag, she was in a state of mild euphoria. Her walk with Blaine Kilcullen around Sydney Harbour's foreshores had been wonderfully exhilarating...

"The best possible way to see Sydney is from the water, of course," he'd explained, with a look of genuine regret. "Unfortunately we don't have time right now. But who knows? Some time in the future...?" He had shifted his dazzling gaze to meet hers. Pinned it as though her eyes held every answer he was looking for.

She had felt excitement ripple down her throat. She might have been a teenager on her first date instead of a sophisticated woman, such had been her feeling of being held spellbound. She'd been increasingly aware he was having that effect on her. Surely it was an unfair advantage? And he'd had it from the first moment, when she'd walked towards him quite calmly when her thoughts had actually been chaotic. She had never expected this. She had never met a man to match him.

She had pretended to brush a strand of hair from her forehead. "I'm only sorry I didn't have time to unpack my camera. This is a truly beautiful city."

"It is that," he agreed. "I've travelled the world, but nothing beats the natural beauty of this harbour. We'll start our tour with the Harbour Bridge. It's the most logical point. It has a pedestrian footpath, and the south-east pylon is a great vantage point for spectacular views of the city, the Opera House and the Harbour. Come along now, Sienna."

He took her arm in gentlemanly fashion, but he might have grabbed her such was the heat of contact. It sizzled through her body. She only hoped he wasn't monitoring her reactions. She would die of mortification. In a way her meeting the cattle baron seemed quite unreal. Or surreal?

A beautiful cruise liner was moored at the Sydney Cove Terminal—the same location, Blaine told her, taken by the ships of the First Fleet when they dropped anchor in the cove in

January 1788. As they stood together companionably and watched another big liner approached. One of the Harbour's "jetcats", on its way out from Circular Quay to Manly on the other side of the Harbour, was passing Sydney Opera House—an unforgettable sight. Its iconic white sails glittered in the brilliant sunlight, the three sides of the World Heritage listed building surrounded by sparkling blue water.

"You probably know it was the renowned Danish architect Jorn Utzon's design." Blaine glanced down on her face, one side half hidden by the dip of her very attractive straw hat. She looked as cool and delicious as ice cream. "Although Utzon's splendid vision was chosen, the irony was that the design was beyond the engineering capabilities of the time. It took Utzon a few years to work out his problems while the costs were blowing out monumentally. There was a stage when the NSW government was tempted to call a halt."

"Thank goodness they didn't!" Sienna exclaimed. "It's a magnificent construction. I would say to a Canadian this is the most recognizable image of Australia."

He nodded. "It's site reaching out into the Harbour makes the building even more spectacular. Utzon must have been thrilled when he heard his design had been chosen. What a site for his building! Could any architect ask for more? There are around a quarter of a million guided tours for visitors every year. Again, we must wait for another time. I'd like to take you to see the Royal Botanic Gardens as they're only a short walk away. I have the feeling you love gardens?"

"Who doesn't?"

"Not all would have your eye for beauty, I imagine, Sienna. Sydney is fortunate to have a thirty-hectare oasis right in the heart of the city. There's a walkway around the harbourfront at the lower part of the gardens we can take."

"What a breathtakingly beautiful setting!" She knew a part of her euphoria was her enormous pleasure in his company, the stimulating way he pointed out everything of interest along with its historical context. She was more than happy with their tour.

"The gardens themselves are splendid, as you will see," Blaine said. "Not tiring on me, are you?' He tipped the brim of her hat so his eyes could move over her face.

He appeared to focus on her every feature in turn. It was stunningly sensual. "Do I look it?" she asked, a faint catch in her voice.

He shot her a sideways smile. "You're the most beautiful woman I've ever seen."

"That sounds faintly mocking."

He laughed. "Also a woman to be approached with a good deal of care."

"And yet here we are!" she challenged.

"And making quite a connection," he offered dryly. "It's very liberating, not having to worry about anything else but enjoying one another's company."

Impossible to disagree. "You *knew* I'd come to Australia, didn't you?" she asked, sweeping off her wide-brimmed hat and fanning herself with it.

"I have to admit it," he said. "You're not going to tell me you're sorry?" Very gently, like a brush of velvet, he reached out to tuck a loose strand of her amber hair behind her ear.

"No way!" It was a measure of how dazzled she was that she gave a little shiver. She was beginning to fear her physical reaction to him—this crazy, near uncontrollable desire for him to touch her. It was a reason for considerable concern. But there it was. And not much she could do about it. "I'm not sure I can predict what's ahead of us, however," she said, a sigh escaping her.

He took her hand and tugged her along almost playfully. "It's enough you're here, Sienna," he said.

She was destined to remember that precise moment for a long, long time…

They flew into the Kilcullen desert stronghold towards late afternoon. It had been a smooth, uneventful flight—although Amanda had professed her nervousness of light aircraft.

"They crash all the time."

"A bit extreme, Amanda," Blaine had soothed her. "You'll be perfectly safe with me. Flying is a way of life in the Outback."

On their flight to the vast arid lands of the remote south-west he had shown himself to be an excellent pilot. Now he was flying low over Katajangga station, so they could get a closer look at the incredible landscape beneath them.

Sienna's whole body seemed to be atremble, with a mix of exhaustion and excitement. It was bringing goosebumps to her bare arms. She wanted to wake Amanda, so she wouldn't miss out on their momentous arrival. Katajangga Station the great land mass that lay beneath her, appeared as a fairly large settlement of many buildings, constructed in an area of absolute wilderness. There was no other sign of human habitation to the horizon—only herds of cattle in holding yards, and thousands of head roaming free across the plains, bisected by fiery red sand dunes that ran in almost exact parallel lines.

Blaine thought better of waking Amanda. "Let her sleep," he advised. "She needs sleep badly."

Sienna turned her head towards her sleeping cousin. Amanda was curled up, looking little more than a child, she thought with a pang of the heart. Amanda would always be her little cousin who had so tragically lost her parents. To compound Amanda's trauma she had now lost her husband, in one mindless act of bravado, even if it appeared her marriage had been well and truly on the rocks. Hadn't the family feared it would happen sooner or later? But when Amanda wanted something she wanted it right away, allowing no time for thought. What she had wanted was a *man*. Not a father figure—that would have been easy enough to understand—but a man to keep her close. No woman could possibly offer her the right reassurance, let alone the sense of being cocooned. Amanda had a rather worrying history of attachments that came unstuck when she became too clingy. According to Mark— probably an excuse for his own behaviour—she had got to that point overnight.

"It's got nothing to do with love, Sienna. Mandy suffocates a man like some parasitic vine."

Loyal as she was to Amanda, she had to recognize the essential truth in that statement.

Sienna blew out a small breath of air. "So why do *I* feel so good?" she asked the cattle baron.

"Now, that's a question," he said in a lightly mocking voice. "I'm awed by your energy." Quite true. Her physical fitness added another dimension to her beauty, making it so much more compelling.

"So am I," she laughed. "It's a mystery to me."

She stared out at the western sky. Such a spectacle was unfolding before her—a spectacle growing more glorious by the minute. "Just look at that sunset! From sapphire-blue crystal to *this*!"

On the western horizon incandescent clouds were building: crimson, bright pink deepening into rose, streaks of palest green, molten gold. To her fascinated eye, a silvery cyclamen ring appeared to surround the pulsing setting sun.

"You'll see plenty of those," Blaine told her with a casual white smile.

"I had thought to see a great *brown* land. This is the most ancient continent on earth, after all. How do I go about describing the colours? There's so much unexpected *green*—especially the dense borders along the water courses. It's like a giant maze of wetlands, with streams and lakes."

"Billabongs, we call them," Blaine said, briefly turning his head. "Billabongs, lagoons, clay pans. Plenty of lignum swamps—that is to say eucalypt wooded swamps. What we call the Mulga Lands. The trees can be more than forty feet high. They have lots of hollows that provide shelter and breeding sites for anything from mammals through reptiles to frogs and waterbirds. What you're seeing is far from the norm. But we've had the best rainfall for many long drought-stricken years."

"Hence all the flowing water?"

He nodded. "The Channel Country is actually a series of ancient flood plains. Most years the rains are soaked into the earth and evaporate. But this rainfall has been so heavy, with flooding intensified by heavy monsoonal rains coming down from the tropical North, that flood waters are flowing into Lake Eyre—which you might know as the largest salt water lake in the world. It only fills up about two or three times in a century." He laughed briefly. "We have a group of eccentrics called the Lake Eyre Yacht Club, who set sail on the lake when it's in flood. They're there right now."

"Truly? What fun! I'd love to see it."

"Maybe you will." He cast her another one of his glittering glances. The ones that nearly stopped her breath.

She had to wait a moment to clear her head. "Didn't Sir Donald Campbell attempt a land-speed record on Lake Eyre, or am I wrong about that?"

Blaine too was feeling little darts of excitement that pierced his skin. He was having seriously divergent thoughts about this beautiful young woman. He felt a certain lack of trust, like watching a sleeping serpent, coiled around a spinifex bush yet always ready to strike. And at the other extreme the deepest possible pleasure in her company. She looked entirely innocent of any wrongdoing in connection with Mark, yet his gut feeling told him he had to face the possibility she was lying—or at the very least hiding their connection. There were fine distinctions between married men and single men. Had she bothered to make them? Whatever the character flaws in Mark, he'd never had any trouble attracting women. And Mark, when he had been focused strongly on something, had made it his business to have it.

Blaine knew he would have to separate the truth from the lies. Her voice released him from his disturbing thoughts.

"I take it I'm wrong?"

"No, you're absolutely right." He was somewhat surprised she knew about the extraordinary Sir Donald, let alone his attempts on Lake Eyre. "The *Bluebird-Proteus*. My father and my grandfather were spectators at that event on the salt flats. The Channel Country lies in the Lake Eyre basin. They were there, too, when Sir Donald broke the speed record on water at Lake Dumbleyung in West Australia. Just over 276 miles per hour. He won the land and the water speed record in the same year. Quite a feat! According to my father, Sir Donald had charisma in spades—a great bloke, but he wouldn't have anyone wish him good luck. He hated it. Apparently he was very superstitious. Sadly, but I suppose not unexpectedly, he died at the wheel a few years later. He was only around forty-five, I believe. There are some photos of him at the house you might like to see."

"I certainly would. What a connection!"

"Over the years we've had plenty of VIPs stay at the station," he said, turning his head to her.

All of a sudden they seemed disturbingly close. She had the feeling he was about to say something, then thought better of it. Either way, her heart was beating high and light in her breast. She did the wise thing. She turned her attention back to the infinite landscape. "It's daunting, isn't it? I'd hate to get lost down there."

"You'd never get out alive," he told her dryly. "Probably our most famous explorer, the great Ludwig Leichhardt, a German, disappeared down there in 1848, along with his entire party of men and animals. He was attempting to cross the continent from east to west. He'd already concluded a triumphal three-thousand-mile journey from Brisbane to Coburg Peninsula, north-east of Darwin in the tropics. But the desert brought him to his death. What happened to Leichhardt is one of the great mysteries of the Outback. Our Nobel Prize winning author Patrick White wrote a book based on him, called *Voss*. There are several copies at the house if you want to read it."

"I'd like to," she said, thoroughly intrigued. "Surely search parties were sent out to find him?"

"Of course—several. But all of them failures. Only a couple of trees marked 'L'. What Leichhardt saw, as you're seeing now, is some of the most rugged country on the planet. But it's also the home of the cattle kings. We produce the best beef."

"So I've read. We also have a thriving beef industry in Canada.'

He nodded. "Large-scale cattle and sheep

ranching in Alberta—the Canadian Texas, don't they say? But think of its huge oil reserves! Has to make it one of the most financially important places on earth. Our traditional beef markets have been the USA and Japan, but Canada is a notable export destination, along with South-East Asia. Both our countries experience the same problems with enormous distances to get the product to market. We use huge road trains here in the Outback—and as you know, we call your ranches stations."

"Yes." She nodded. "I've been doing a little research for the trip. It's a very British term—*station.*"

"Well, it would be. All of our historic stations, sheep and cattle, were founded by men of vision and adventure from the United Kingdom—including my own forebears. You have a French background?"

"Very much so. Sometimes fiercely so. My father's family hail from Quebec, easily the most Francophile province. My mother's family has been long settled in BC. They actually met in New York, at an art showing. My father loves British Columbia—its beautiful landscapes, the

Rockies and the forests. My parents are long divorced, but they both still live in Vancouver. Dad travels widely, of course, but Vancouver is home."

"I expect he wants to be near his daughter."

"We're very close." She gave him a quick smile, her gaze returning to the gigantic landscape. "I did read about the wild flowers after rain, but I never expected to see the land awash with them on my arrival. That's incredible." Below her, vast areas were covered in white wild flowers, adjacent areas were yellow, with big areas of pink mixed with purple, and only small spaces of the rust-red carpet of earth in between.

"I stress you're seeing the *good* times," Blaine said. "The entire character of the landscape has been transformed by 'the white and golden glory of the daisy-patterned plains,' to quote one of our Outback poets. The yellow and white are all paper daisies—everlastings. Bachelor buttons, we call them. The pink and pale green areas are *parakeelyas*—succulents the cattle can feed on. The divine blessing of rain has truly been with us. As an artist, you're seeing our Channel Country at its very best. Though I would have preferred for you and Amanda to see it at a less grievous time, naturally. Hilary will be waiting to greet you. Marcia too, of course. You didn't tell Amanda about Joanne?"

Sienna shook her head. "The timing didn't seem right. I take it Joanne will be at the funeral?"

"Joanne and her entire family," he said. "But don't worry about Joanne. She was very deeply hurt, but she knows how to behave."

"And are you asking me if *Amanda* can do the same?" she responded with a challenge.

"Sort of." He kept his voice impassive. "She's in shock—as she would be. Aside from the long flights, she doesn't appear to be coping all that well."

"Why would she be? She's in a deep state of shock. But there's something that bothers me," she confessed.

"Let's have it." He flashed his diamond-hard glance at her.

Instead of freezing her out, it had the opposite effect, spreading a trail of sizzling warmth. The two of them were cut off from the rest of the world. It seemed the most remarkable thing to be with him at all—like a dream sequence. "You've spoken of how Mark mentioned me in his letter to his mother," she began tentatively, "telling her of his marriage?"

"Is there something else?" he asked, more sternly than he'd intended.

"Something else?" She felt a jolt of simple despair. "There you go again. Of course there isn't something else. I'm concerned she too may have the wrong impression."

"Maybe Mark had a huge crush on you," he suggested, with another searing glance.

"Hardly likely, when he was marrying someone else—my cousin Amanda." She injected outrage into her voice, all the more because it was shockingly true.

"Who knows with poor old Mark?" The expression on his dynamic face darkened. Who knew what secret sins? Betrayal? Adultery with this beautiful creature? She appeared above such behaviour—but a man and a woman? Always temptation. Always was. Always would be. She might be very far from being Mark's "type", but he had no difficulty seeing Mark letting her into his life. Maybe Mark had finally lost his taste for bubble-headed girls.

"You're not thinking straight, Blaine!" she warned him.

"No?" He fixed his eyes on her.

She couldn't look away. Usually she was adept in controlling man-woman situations. Not with him.

"There's not a man alive who couldn't be caught up in the web a beautiful, highly intelligent woman can spin."

"Oh, yes, there is," she returned with biting sarcasm. *"You."*

When this was all over she might just collapse and have a good cry. For now she had to be strong for Amanda. She had to see her cousin through this traumatic trip to meet her late husband's family. The smartest thing she could do for herself was keep a strong defensive wall in place. She recognized the powerful dangers of getting to know this dark and edgy cattle baron any better. She would be wise not to expose herself to those dangers.

They made a perfect touch down ten minutes later. "We're here at last!" Sienna cried, unable to fully contain her excitement.

"Welcome to Katajangga," Blaine said, taxiing the Beech Baron towards a huge silver hangar.

"This is unlike anything I've ever seen! A small country town in the middle of an endless ocean of red sand and rioting miles of wild flowers."

He had to admit her enthusiasm was giving him an adrenalin shot of pleasure. But then she was an artist, with a finely honed eye for beauty in all its forms. "Glad you like it," he said. "How are *you* feeling, Amanda?" he asked, with a half-turn of his head.

"Exhausted," she croaked, starting to sit up straight.

"You'll feel a whole lot better when you've caught up with your sleep."

"I hope so. I feel dizzy and nauseous. I must look a fright."

"Just a little pale," Sienna said.

A flash of the bitter, irrational resentment that had plagued Amanda for most of her life surfaced before Amanda had time to recall it. "Oh, shut up, Sienna," she said resentfully. "We can't all look like *you*."

No, indeed! Blaine made no comment on Amanda's rudeness, but he privately agreed.

Sienna, despite their long travels, somehow managed to look as fresh as a rose.

He had long awaited his meeting with Mark's widow, but now he realized she was a young woman with serious issues. Not the least of them jealousy of her cousin. He had taken account of the way she practically bit Sienna's head off every time she opened her mouth. In fact there was something of a manic edge about Amanda that put him in mind of his half-brother. The odd time, however, Amanda showed considerable dependence upon her cousin. So there she was, sending out an ambivalent set of signals.

Love-hate. Sometimes the strong suffered poor treatment from the more vulnerable members of a family, Blaine mused. There had always been tremendous strain between him and Mark, though he had tried his level best to be as supportive as he knew how. Only Mark had chafed endlessly at what he saw as his secondary status. It was emerging Sienna was suffering a fate similar to his own.

The sun, having turned on another glorious display for the day, was sinking fast onto the horizon, leaving a lovely mauve world. It was one of the colours Sienna would always associate with the Outback. They were being met by a station employee, a rangy individual, running the brim of his akubra through his fingers and saying, "G'day!" before driving them to the homestead— a good mile from the hangar that housed the Beech Baron and what looked like a state-of-the-art dark grey helicopter. Two yellow helicopters sat on the broad concrete apron. Sienna assumed correctly they were used for mustering.

They drove along a broad gravel track bordered by soaring gums. Ahead was a terracotta wall some eight feet high. It was draped in the long overhanging arms of a prolific flowering vine, with masses and masses of cerise blossom that made a dramatic splash of colour. Bougainvillea. In the wall a massive black wrought-iron gate stood open. Flanking it were two magnificent date palms such as Sienna had always associated with the deserts of the Middle East.

"The wall is to protect the homestead from dust storms," Blaine threw over his shoulder. "And to protect the garden too, of course. Hilary loves her garden. It's a dry region garden, watered by sunken bores. We're over the Great Artesian Basin. We couldn't survive without it. Don't worry about any lengthy greetings tonight, Amanda. Everyone appreciates you'll be exhausted after so much travelling. A hello, then you'll be shown your room. Anything you want to eat will be sent up to you. Okay?"

"Thank you for being so thoughtful, Blaine." Amanda leaned forward in her seat to say sweetly, "You're coming with me, aren't you, Sienna?"

Sienna shook her head. "I'm not ready for bedtime yet." Her fascinated gaze was on the fortified Katajangga homestead. It made her think of some wonderful hidden desert retreat. The sky was darkening to purple, so the interior and exterior lights were turned on. She could hear the cooling sound of running water. Where better than from a splendid stone fountain that was the focal point in the enclosed courtyard? Light caught the water, forming rainbows. It splashed and cascaded over three graduating basins held aloft by rearing horses with flowing manes into the circular pond beneath.

Her eyes ranged over the soaring palms to flowering shrubs she recognized as oleanders. Their heady perfume permeated the air. In triangular boxed beds grew great sunbursts of ornamental spiky grasses. In other beds the gigantic leaf rosettes of Mexican agaves. Both species would resist a searing desert sun. In different places a range of boulders lent a stunning sculptural effect.

"This is a magical place," she said, with genuine delight.

"You ought to dress up as a sheikh, Blaine," Amanda suggested, not wanting to be left out. He would make a gorgeous sheikh. So dark and so damned sexy!

"I think I'll stick to being a cattle man," he said. "But, speaking of sheikhs—or dress-up sheikhs—I've seen some garments worn by Lawrence of Arabia in the Canberra war museum. The caftan would be about your size, Sienna. He must have been a very slim, small man, with big ideas."

"But, hey, Peter O'Toole was *tall*!" Amanda piped up with this *non sequitur*. "We'll have to smother ourselves in sunblock, Sienna. It's evening, but I can still feel the heat in my skin."

"We'll look after you, Amanda," Blaine assured her, relieved she was sounding a little more cheerful. One aspect puzzling him was that Amanda gave off no real sense of grief. In fact he didn't identify her with the image of a grieving widow at all. He had to compare Hilary, on the terrible day of his father's funeral, sedated and held together for a short while, before the inevitable collapse. Hilary had idolized his father.

"I cannot imagine how I'm going to get through life without him, Blaine."

At the time he'd felt pretty much the same thing—grief at the loss of a beloved parent and life mentor; the shock of being catapulted into one tough job many years in advance.

Sienna, catching his expression, wondered what he was thinking. Probably he had already formed his opinion of them both. Amanda, Mark's widow, who wasn't displaying much in the way of sorrow; and her, the shadowy figure in the background, who might or might not have embarked on some sort of affair with her own cousin's husband.

Anyone who knew her would know there wasn't a skerrick of truth in it.

Blaine Kilcullen didn't know her at all.

CHAPTER FOUR

KATAJANGGA homestead fitted perfectly into its extraordinary desert landscape. Like the massive fortifying walls, the stone house had been rendered and washed with a deep terracotta colour. There was a two-storey central section, with a hipped metal roof and a long run of covered deck supported by massive stacked stone pillars, and a central core flanked by single-storey wings set at a forty-five degree angle from the main house. Sienna guessed these were additions that had evolved over time, turning the original homestead into something quite grand.

"I'm going to be sick," Amanda muttered out of the side of her mouth.

"No, you're not!" Firmly Sienna took hold of her cousin's small hand. "No one will be expecting you to do much talking. We'll be greeted, and then, as Blaine says, we'll be shown to our rooms."

Amanda posted a clear warning. "They'd better be nice to me."

Sienna pressed her hand supportively. "Everyone wants to be nice to you, Mandy. Just remember to be nice to *them*."

There was no entrance hall, as such, but the Great Room was spectacular for its sheer size alone. It took in almost the length and breadth of the house, with staircases leading to the upper floor on the extreme left and right. There was a massive ceiling-high fireplace made of slabs of stone, big and small, wide-planked timber floors with a dark stained glossy patina, comfortable seating areas arranged around the room, and an area for dining with a mahogany table that could easily seat twenty or more. Splendid rugs with muted desert colours and elements of Asia lent an exotic touch. She was familiar with the arts of Asia. Her own beautiful British Columbia boasted the largest Asian population outside Asia, and her mother had a magnificent collection of Chinese porcelains and jades. A decorative timber railing enclosed an upper gallery, which Sienna could see was hung with paintings.

In many ways the interior was like that of a

huge prairie house, except for the great crystal chandeliers that instead of appearing incongruous captured the imagination. She knew there had to be a story to those antique chandeliers. They were as beautiful and extravagant as she had ever seen.

Amanda too was staring about her, her blonde head tilted to the gallery which overhung the Great Room by ten or more feet. "Where is everybody?" she asked, one minute desperate to dodge Mark's family, the next put out that there was no welcoming party.

Before Sienna could formulate a single word— nervous about what Amanda might say next—a tall, middle-aged woman in a dark blue dress, with a wealth of greying hair almost to her shoulders, suddenly appeared to their left.

"Ah, here's Hilary now," Blaine said. He waited a moment to see if Marcia had accompanied her mother and was hanging back. No such luck, even though Hilary's deep suffering would have aroused pity in the hardest heart.

Hilary approached them, holding out her hand. "You, of course, are Amanda," she said in a soft wavery voice, her eyes fixed on Amanda's pretty face and petite figure.

"I am," said Amanda, her graciousness all dried up.

Blaine stood back so he could observe this long overdue meeting. Amanda made no move to go into her mother-in-law's arms, although it was painfully obvious that was what Hilary wanted and perhaps expected.

Sienna too stood well back, in deference to her cousin. Amanda didn't like being touched and was making that apparent. Not even a smile!

"Welcome to Katajangga, my dear," Hilary was saying. "We are so grateful you could make the long journey."

"I fully planned to," Amanda lied. She submitted to a handshake with a look of surprise on her face she didn't bother to hide. *This* was Mark's mother? What a turn-up! No matriarchal figure here. Not by a long shot. She was no looker, either. In fact she was downright plain—and that wavery voice! Hilary was a far cry from the handsome, intimidating woman Amanda had conjured up in her mind. According to Mark his mother had always been very tough on him. She had failed him, letting him down, siding with her husband and Blaine.

"A traitor she is, my mother!"

Amanda was seriously astonished, and at the same time relieved. This woman would be a pushover. And she looked so *old* when she couldn't be. Aunt Francine, for instance, at fifty, looked marvellous!

Blaine watched his frail stepmother turn to Sienna. "And you must be Sienna," she said, with a heart-wrenching smile.

"How do you do, Mrs Kilcullen?"

He watched with critical appraisal as Sienna stepped forward. She was now beneath the direct light of a chandelier that set her glorious hair on fire. He saw her take his stepmother's thin hand, not in a conventional handshake but in what appeared to him to be a warm clasp. "It's a pleasure to meet you," she said, in a charming voice that had a gentle *hush* to it as she addressed Hilary. "I only wish the circumstances weren't so very, very sad. Please allow me to offer my deepest sympathy."

Blaine found himself releasing a taut breath. In truth, he was enormously grateful Sienna had

had the sensitivity to read the lines of suffering on Hilary's face, the double dose of tragedy and her subsequent grief.

To Sienna's surprise Hilary reached out and patted her cheek. "Sometimes really bad things can lead to good things, my dear," she said. "You're very welcome here, Sienna. Please, do call me Hilary." There had only ever been one Mrs Kilcullen, and that had been Blaine's late mother, Hilary thought—entirely without rancour.

With a hint of impatience Amanda jerked her blonde head up once more, looking to the gallery. "Where's Marcia? I'd like to meet her. I suppose she looks just like Mark?"

Blaine cut in smoothly. "Not all that much, Amanda. They're not identical twins. But there are many likenesses you can decide on tomorrow. Marcia is giving you time to settle in. Isn't that so, Hilary?" He looked towards his stepmother.

His glittering light eyes highlighted the black of his hair and brows and the polished bronze of his skin, Sienna noticed. She was fully aware that Amanda and she were under close scrutiny. Like Amanda, she was surprised by Hilary Kilcullen's appearance and the shyness of her manner. But she found it understandable, given the deep grief Hilary must be suffering. Perhaps her life's role as the second Mrs Kilcullen hadn't been much of a confidence-booster.

Hilary picked up on Blaine's hint, grateful as ever for her stepson's unending support. "We knew you'd be desperately tired."

"Actually, I'm not as tired as I would have thought," Sienna said in some surprise. "I expect it will hit me tomorrow."

"Then perhaps you would join us for dinner?" Hilary turned to Sienna eagerly, looking her full in the face. She was feeling far more comfortable with Amanda's cousin than with her son's widow. Amanda was very pretty, or she would be when she was rested, but her cousin—*the bridesmaid*—was uncommonly beautiful, with extraordinary colouring and a grace of manner. Even more importantly, Hilary knew instinctively this young woman was genuinely kind.

She recalled in detail every word her son had written about his wife's bridesmaid. At the time she and Blaine had found it extremely puzzling, but she didn't find it puzzling now. Mark had found a woman—not his wife—who had deeply moved him. Mark, who was no longer with them. Mark, who would be buried in two days' time.

A big blonde woman—not fat, but solid—came down the staircase to the left. She crossed the polished timber floor to where they were assembled.

"This is Magda." Hilary introduced their housekeeper with a fond smile. "Magda runs the house for us. Most efficiently, I should add. Magda, this is Amanda, Mark's wife, and her cousin Sienna."

Magda nodded her large blonde head in what was intended to be a salute. "Please to come with me," she said in a strong, deep voice, feminine none the less. It still held the trace of a Polish accent. "I will show you to your rooms."

"Thank you, Magda." Blaine took over from his stepmother. "Dinner is at seven if you feel up to it," he addressed Sienna.

"Don't worry. We're going to crash," Amanda cut in, her feathers already ruffled. The limelight that should be on *her* had shifted to Sienna.

Yet *again*.

They moved down a long grand corridor in the tall housekeeper's wake. Magda showed Amanda into her room first. The large, elegant guest room with its soft hues and furnishings was intended for a woman, Sienna thought, following the other two in. A big, romantic four-poster bed immediately caught the eye. It was placed between ceiling-high timber doors that led out onto a balcony that would have views over the extensive rear grounds. She caught glimpses of tall palms. The palette was predominantly blue and white, and a dazzling abstract flower painting hung over the bed to liven things up. She would have liked to study it further. It didn't look European. Aboriginal? There was a pretty desk and chair, and some exceptional pieces of furniture—a daybed upholstered in blue silk, with two matching armchairs.

"This is lovely!' she said, always one to make a warm remark. Amanda, however, was embarrassing her by appearing more than a tad underwhelmed. Where had her good manners gone? Sienna agonized. She had to take into account that Amanda was exhausted, but she hoped her cousin would pick up for the remainder of their stay. There was the funeral to face; doubtless a wake to follow. And, God help them, there was Mark's ex-fiancée, Joanne, to confront. And her parents. Plus all the friends of the Kilcullen family. Most probably it would be a huge affair.

"I will show you to your room now, Ms Sienna," said Magda, pivoting surprisingly lightly on her rubber-soled shoes.

"Thank you, Magda. Do you want to come and see, Amanda?" Sienna asked.

But Amanda was sucking in her cheeks. A familiar mannerism. "I can see it tomorrow," she said flatly. "Can you help me unpack? I tell you, I'm *whacked*."

"Of course you are," Sienna soothed. "I'll come back."

"Is my job to do unpacking," Magda intervened.

"I prefer my cousin," Amanda replied, like a rude child. "And I will want something to eat."

"It will be done," said Magda, showing no sign of disapproval at Amanda's sulky schoolgirl retort.

Sienna's room, two doors down along the wide painting-hung corridor, was very different. For one thing the colour scheme might have been designed with her specifically in mind.

"Thank you, Magda. I'll be very comfortable here," she said, smiling at the housekeeper.

"Mr Blaine chose your room," Magda replied. "It is *sunshine*." She threw out her arms.

"It *is*." Sienna felt a quick lift of the heart, like a bird taking wing. *Blaine* had personally chosen which room she was to have? Like Amanda's room, there was a centrepiece four-poster bed, but hers was ebony, with brass finials and a hand-painted gold trim. Not surprisingly with her colouring, she loved the colour yellow—which had been used generously in the beautiful room. The bedcover and pillows were of yellow silk, but there was a tangerine, scarlet and gold coverlet lying at the foot of the bed. A single yellow rose stood in a vase, beneath a lamp on the small bedside table.

"Dressing room and bathroom beyond." Magda gestured. "Would you like me to unpack, Ms Sienna?" she asked, indicating the two pieces of luggage that now stood at Sienna's door.

"That would be lovely, Magda." Sienna would have preferred to do the unpacking herself, but she was anxious not to offend the housekeeper. She had spotted the fact that Magda was something of a personage in the household, and very probably indispensable to Hilary.

"I'll do it now, while you comfort Mrs Kilcullen," Magda said.

"My cousin has never been a good traveler." Sienna thought an excuse was in order. "I'll find out for you what she would like to eat. I think *I'll* have dinner downstairs. I have my own methods of getting over jet lag. Thank you, Magda."

When she returned to Amanda's room she found her cousin lying limply on the four-poster bed. Sienna turned back to shut the heavy door and block any sound.

"What are you *doing*?" Amanda lifted her head in amazement.

"Shutting the door—obviously," Sienna said. "Anyone would think I was locking you in a prison cell. Magda is just down the corridor, unpacking for me." Mandy was turning into something of a loose cannon.

Amanda choked on a dry laugh. "It makes you happy, doesn't it—sucking everyone in?"

"It would make me a lot happier if *you'd* try," Sienna retorted.

"I can't try. Not *now*." Amanda's large blue eyes welled with tears.

Sienna sank down onto the bed, pushing away

her own irritations. "Mandy, I know you're grieving *inside*, but Blaine and Mark's mother could be missing it. They don't know you like I do."

"So you want me to shed buckets all over them?" Amanda was pushing her loose wedding ring and diamond solitaire engagement ring rather manically up and down on her finger. "Mark didn't love me. End of story. End of grieving. The man didn't love me."

"Did you love *him*, Mandy?" Sienna asked very quietly. "I mean really love him? Not the sex."

Amanda stared up at the ceiling. "I've been thinking a lot about that. It's like you once said to me— 'Mandy, you fall in love with *love*, but love means committing to one person.' I know what you're going to say. I *committed* all over the place. Maybe I was a bit promiscuous—which you did your best to hide from the family. So thanks for that. Anyway, I don't want to talk about Mark. Our marriage broke up long ago. *You* know."

"You'll never abandon your groundless accusations, will you?" Sienna asked with weary resignation. "Better to blame someone other than yourself. You might want to think long and hard about where *you* went wrong instead of always trying to fix the blame on me."

"Okay, okay!" Amanda cried, extending a conciliatory hand to Sienna, who took it from long habit. "So what's with the housekeeper?" she asked. "God, she's nearly as tall as Blaine."

"She is tall, yes. But she's rather a fine-looking woman. Mandy, you need to consider that Magda is an important person around here."

Amanda rolled her eyes. "You're joking! The housekeeper? *Important*?"

"Believe it," Sienna said. "Now, what would you like sent up on a tray?"

"You're *not* going downstairs?" Amanda cast Sienna's hand away, as though deeply disappointed in her. "You're *not* leaving me?"

"No need to get worked up." Sienna rose to her feet. "My metabolism is clearly different from yours. I'll have dinner, then an early night."

"Don't give that!" Amanda snorted in disgust. "It's Blaine, isn't it? I mean, he's a *really* sensational guy."

Sienna just smiled. "With, I expect, a conga line of suitable prospective wives lined up. Why wouldn't he—a man like that?"

"Maybe you're after a fling?" Amanda's blue gaze was as sharp as a razor.

Sienna started to walk to the door. "I don't go in for flings, remember?"

"No, you're such a self-righteous person—always in control. But you haven't met a guy like this to date."

"This conversation is entirely inappropriate, Amanda," Sienna said. "We're here to bury Mark, remember? It's a sad and solemn occasion."

"Sure it is!" Amanda snapped. "But *my* legacy as Mark's widow is the *big* deal." She thrust her curly blonde head back into the pillows, folding her arms across her chest. "What do you reckon I'll get?"

"Mandy, I wouldn't know."

"Better be substantial," Amanda said. "These people are filthy rich. If I'm not happy with what I'm offered I'm going to demand more."

Sienna turned back, appalled. "I wouldn't go *demanding* anything of Blaine Kilcullen, Amanda. It would be a big mistake. Can't you see how tough he is?"

Amanda smiled up at the ceiling. "I love the way he kinda *smoulders*," she said. "Mark always did say he was ruthless. Anyway, enough of that. What I'd really like to eat is a burger with fries. No ketchup. A glass or two of white wine. They should be able to rise to that."

"That's not much of a choice," Sienna said.

"*My* choice, sweetie. I think they were lying about Marcia. I don't think she wants to meet us."

Sienna didn't answer, but she supposed Amanda might very well be right.

The day of the funeral.

Since her arrival Sienna had found it impossible to sleep in. The light woke her, and the tremendous outpouring of birdsong—such a melodious din she thought the rising sun might still be surprised by it. Today was one of brilliant sunshine. Golden rays were already starting to slant across the wide timber deck with its fifteen-foot overhang. No tears from heaven for Mark, she thought. She turned on her back, seeking solace in the birds' piercingly sweet music played at a full *fortissimo*. Now and again the sweetness was underscored by a loud cackling—no other word for it—that cut through the orchestration.

She would carry the memory of this wild bush chorus for a very long time.

Moments later she rose, pulling on her pale pink satin robe, leaving the sash untied. Strangely enough, the highly irritable Amanda slept through the dawn orchestra—which was all to the good for today. Amanda's mood swings were legendary. She hoped and prayed they would get through the day without incident. Releasing her long hair from its loose night-time plait, she let it slide over her shoulder, padding across the carpet and out onto the huge deck. It ran the entire length of the first floor, with rattan and bamboo outdoor settings at intervals. The double rooms were screened to some extent by the graceful sweep of palm fronds from the palms growing in huge Asian planters.

At this time in the morning the atmosphere was pleasantly cool, although she knew it would soon build up to real heat. The scents from the extensive open garden were incredibly heady, even hectic, compared to what she was used to. Sweetness mingled with strong aromatic and citrus-type perfumes. The rear garden was a virtual oasis, with a meandering route through banks and banks of small flowering trees and amazingly colourful bushes. The fragrance from the white and violet lilies used as a massed bedding plant wafted to her easily. The lilies were unfamiliar to her. She supposed they were native, since they were thriving so lavishly in such dry conditions.

Moving across to the timber railing, she held onto it with both hands, allowing the glory of the morning to soothe her troubled spirits. Mindful of the day ahead, she closed her eyes and tilted her head to the sapphire sky.

Please God, keep us from harm. Show mercy to Mark. Show mercy to us all. Get Mandy safely through this sad day...

That was how Blaine came on her. He was transfixed by the sight. He even felt a charge in the air. He had to be aware his usual tight control was slipping further and further with this woman. At this hour, and after their long flight, he hadn't expected to see sight nor sign of his guests. They would be sleeping in, gathering their strength for the day ahead. He'd been tucking his bush shirt into his jeans as he'd walked to the French doors of the master suite, glancing out on the day and wondering what it might bring.

Since his father had died he had moved into what had traditionally been the master suite; prior to that he had occupied the entire west wing, which he still retained. Hilary, quite naturally, on her marriage had not wanted the suite of rooms always associated with his mother, the first Mrs Kilcullen, mistress of Katajangga. She had chosen the next largest room. There were seven double bedrooms strung along this upper floor. In the old days they'd always had plenty of guests, some of them important people. These days Hilary and Marcia occupied the east wing.

Moving into the master suite had somehow made him feel closer to the mother he had lost. That was the telling thing. To lose a parent when young, especially a mother, had the after effects playing over and over right through one's life. He had never hated Hilary, who had supplanted his mother. How could anyone hate Hilary? But it had taken him many years to warm to her. Now, thankfully, they were close.

Even from a distance he could see Sienna's lips moving. He sensed she was saying some prayer on this day of days. For Mark? For poor, troubled Mark to be at rest? He waited a moment, then on impulse called to her. Maybe he shouldn't have. She was still wearing her nightgown and robe, her long beautiful hair flowing down her back. He would be invading her privacy. But that didn't stop him.

"Sienna?"

He kept his resonant voice low, but it would carry to her ears. The last thing he wanted to do was wake Mark's young widow, who herself was full of demons. Amanda kept mostly to her room, clearly unable to find it in her heart to offer sympathy and support to her mother-in-law, let alone friendliness. Maybe she had good reason not to take to Marcia, who had made her first appearance at yesterday's lunch. Marcia, though polite enough on the surface—he had demanded that of her—had spoken to him afterwards, in one of her private little rages that could be so like Mark's.

"I don't like her, Blaine. She looks like butter wouldn't melt in her mouth, yet you must have noticed she has a serious grudge against Sienna. I bet she's had it for years. Mark let us down. She's let us down. You can bet your life she's here

for the money. I like Sienna. She's very different.
But I don't like or trust Amanda."

Hilary hadn't risked shocking the young, impressionable Marcia by showing her the letter Mark had sent to her after his marriage. For a married man to fall in love with another woman could have terrible consequences. Blaine's instincts told him Mark had been very much in love with or at least torn over his feelings for his wife's bridesmaid. When had Sienna discovered that? For that matter, when exactly had Amanda, his wife, ceased to interest him?

Sienna awaited Blaine's approach with a touch of trepidation. Perversely, she was also revelling in that sense of high excitement and danger he carried with him. He was half dressed, his shirt unbuttoned almost to the waist. She realized he could have worn anything at all and still caught the eyes of women. He had a superb body. One was constantly aware of the musculature beneath his polished bronze skin, just as one would be conscious of the musculature beneath the pelt of a big cat. It added to his already intensely sexual aura. She had never experienced anything approaching what she felt with this man. That alone set off the alarm bells.

"Couldn't sleep?" He reached her, staring down at her, warding off the quite lunatic desire to pull her into his arms. Physically reaching out for her was out of the question. He had thought he could handle just about anything. Hell, he *was* handling a multitude of things. But he was seriously starting to doubt his ability to handle this woman. Her allure was fantastic—that delicate femininity. It was like a gauzy web that whirled around her, drawing him in whether he wanted it or not: another powerful weapon in this beautiful woman's arsenal. No wonder Mark had found her irresistible.

For God's sake, answer. Make your voice work.

Sienna needed that jolt from her inner voice. Even so, she was amazed at the friendly calm of her response. "The birds woke me. I've never heard such a glorious din in my entire life."

He laughed, turning his head away from her to look out over the vast vistas. "In an hour or so the mirage will be up and abroad. As for the birds—they wake me every day of my life."

He risked turning back to look at her. Her skin

in the dazzling morning light was flawless, so lustrous he wanted to stroke it. There were intensities and *intensities* in life, he thought. He'd had his share of relationships, very pleasant for the most part, but the power this woman had was almost a threat. He had known her too short a time, yet he had to strain to maintain some sort of distance between them. At that minute he wanted to pull her to him by her long amber hair. He could see the faint rise and fall of her breasts. Her heartbeat was making the lace that dipped low into her cleavage tremble.

He braced his arms against the railing, making a real effort to recapture distance. "Have you heard the ringnecks yet? You must have. There's a whole colony of them out there." He waved in the direction of the banks of blossoming trees. "They're large birds, mostly emerald-green, with a distinct yellow collar and a red band across the top of their bills."

Sienna followed his lead. She too was at pains to hide how his presence was affecting her. From the very beginning she had sensed the heat in him, the heat he covered with severity, yet perversely it stirred turbulent sexual feelings. "Would they be the ones who give that whistling call when they're in the air?" she asked. "I've never sighted so many parrots."

"This is the land of parrots. Ringnecks can be very boisterous."

Just a jumble of words—a good safe topic when what he was thinking was: *Just you and me.* Neither of them was moving, as though they couldn't bring themselves to do so, yet he knew she found just as much danger as he did in their closeness. He didn't want this woman soothing and exciting him in turn. A man in his position could never keep hold of a woman like that, bred to the high life. It would be like keeping a gorgeous bird of paradise in a cage.

Sienna studied his handsome, resolute profile, sensing the perturbation in him.

"What thoughts were going through your head when I called to you?" he asked.

She took in breath at a rush. "A prayer to get us all through the day. I'm so, so sorry for Hilary. Marcia too, of course. But she's young and in far less pain than Mark's mother."

"You're not sorry for me?"

"You're wonderfully blunt."

"That doesn't answer the question."

"No." She dared to turn her body sideways. His coal-black hair was tousled into deep waves, with one stray lock resting on his broad tanned forehead. The sun was picking up bluish highlights. He looked incredibly vibrant, and as much a man as she could ever imagine. "I *hope* I am."

For some reason that amused him. "You haven't mentioned Amanda, which has to be a bit odd?"

Her sigh was impatient. "I know you're very observant, Blaine, and you've had Amanda and me under close observation from the start. Amanda losing both her parents so young has left its imprint, like a kind of desolation. She wards off pain. She thinks of it as an actual invader. She won't let it in. But the death of someone very close to us, even when we're estranged, always brings pain. Amanda is in her own kind of despair. She and Mark weren't all that happy towards the end. Perhaps the marriage wouldn't have lasted—who knows? But don't judge Amanda too harshly. I know you've been doing that."

"Then how would you have me see her?" he asked tersely. "Mark's mother doesn't exist for her. Marcia either."

"Well, they've been strangers up until now," she countered.

He blew out a derisive breath. "How come *you've* managed to make friends with Hilary and Marcia? Magda too for that matter. You have an amazing physical ease with people. It comes across as pure warmth."

"What do you think it is?" A flash of anger heightened the colour of her eyes.

"A great asset, Sienna," he returned smoothly. "It's very beguiling."

"And you think possibly a learned social skill?"

"Your eyes spark fire when you're angry," he said, looking deeply into them.

"And you enjoy leading me on."

His firm, sensual mouth twitched. "Guilty as charged. Let's call a truce for today. I was only pointing out that Hilary and Marcia, and include Magda, are hoping you'll stay on for a good while."

"But, Blaine, Amanda will want to go home very soon."

He laughed without humour. "What has that got to do with you? Amanda's a grown woman. And she's already raised the subject of money."

That shocked her. "Has she r-r-eally?" she stumbled. "When?" Amanda had never breathed a word.

She was staring up at him, her lovely lips parted. He felt like an explorer who had happened upon a gold mine. Another time he wouldn't have hesitated. He would have pulled her to him and kissed her hard for as long as it took to have her melting in his arms. He wondered if she knew it. He wondered if she would stop him. Only today wasn't the day for a display of serious lust. He had to call it that. *Lust.* Even though he knew it for what it was. A powerful attraction at all levels. Attraction of the mind was as alluring in its way as sexual desire for a woman's body.

"When did she mention it?" Sienna asked again, picking up the sensuality in his expression. Did he see the response that swept through her?

"She found a minute last night." He shrugged.

"She never said a word."

"According to Amanda, *you* advised her it was about time she started speaking up," he said.

She threw back her head. "I absolutely deny that!'

He couldn't withdraw his hand. He reached out

and caught a handful of her thick silky hair. "Oh, dear—you're saying Amanda was telling fibs?" he taunted.

She jerked back, more disturbed by his hand on her hair than Amanda's all too familiar malicious lies. "Believe what you want to believe, Blaine. I know you do. Did she mention how much I'd told her she should expect?"

"Far more than she's going to get."

"Are you serious?" She bridled at his grand, insolent arrogance. Even so she wanted to *touch* him—run her fingers along his clean chiselled jaw…move her fingers to trace his raised lip line… He was more *real* to her than any man she had ever known. She had to internalize that.

"Very serious," he replied.

"Okay, how much does she want?" She threw down the gauntlet, taking an involuntary step nearer.

"A lot less than she first thought." If she took one more step he really would lose it. He watched her flip the long lock of hair he had taken hold of over her shoulder. It rippled sinuously down her back. Beautiful hair truly was a woman's crowning glory, he thought, realizing he would have to proceed very carefully.

"At least you're saying *she*."

"Suppose we stop now," he said. Was it common sense, a natural caution, or every male's inbuilt fear of a woman's power?

Suddenly she looked contrite. "Of course. But you really do like to stir things up."

"*You* play that game best."

Her head came up to stare into his lambent eyes. "I really don't know what you're talking about."

He laughed and turned away. "Give me some credit, Sienna," he said, dry as ash. "By the way, everyone should be here by ten o'clock. Most are flying in. Some will come cross-country. It won't be a big funeral, like Dad's. But we can expect around one hundred people."

"Joanne and her family are coming, as planned?" She suddenly realized the sun must be shining through her satin nightgown. She should have tied the sash, but too late now. It was the tingle of electricity she got with his eyes on her that reined in her will.

"Yes, they are." Blaine speared his fingers into his hair. "Do your best with Amanda."

"What is that supposed to mean?"

"Oh, God, Sienna!" He gave a wholly unexpected groan. "You must have spent years keeping your cousin out of trouble, even if you couldn't stop her marrying Mark. My first thought, my main loyalty, is for Hilary. Losing Dad nearly killed her. Now she has to bury her son. She loved Mark unconditionally. I have to admit I set conditions. Conditions that were never met. I don't want Hilary subjected to any untoward outbursts from Amanda. I'm sorry if it pains you, but I think regular outbursts power Amanda, just like they powered Mark. They had that in common if nothing else."

This Sienna already knew.

She knocked on Amanda's door at around nine o'clock, waiting for her cousin to call for her to come in. Amanda hadn't come down to breakfast. Sienna, Hilary and Marcia had breakfasted together in a surprisingly companionable fashion. Magda had taken a tray up to Amanda.

She was standing in the middle of the room, wearing only her bra and knickers, but she had her make-up on and her freshly washed blonde hair was curling softly around her gamine little face. She looked very pale and peaky, however.

"Feeling a little better?" Sienna asked, with a rush of concern.

"I feel awful, if you must know," Amanda said irritably. "Really nauseous. I threw up my breakfast."

"Good grief." The thought that Amanda might be pregnant sprang into Sienna's mind, but she immediately rejected it. Amanda would have told her.

"Those damned pills the doctor gave me after the accident. They helped, but they don't agree with me."

"You're not supposed to mix medication with alcohol, Mandy," Sienna said, as gently as she could.

"Oh, don't start!" Amanda was at once affronted. "I need it at the moment."

"Okay, just try to relax." Sienna endeavoured to be as soothing as possible. "Where's your dress?" She glanced towards the pretty blue dress lying on the bed. Was Amanda thinking of wearing that?

"I'm not wearing black, like you," Amanda burst out, obviously a bundle of nerves.

"Okay, okay—don't upset yourself. Not today. So you're thinking of wearing the blue? It's a little bit—"

"Mark *loved* me in it." Amanda said, pushing Sienna's efforts at soothing her aside. "He loved me in blue."

"All right. I understand. You don't have to wear black. What about your hat?"

"*What* hat?" Amanda screeched, pouring a overload of bitter resentment into it. "I don't have a hat." She flopped into an armchair, looking very tense and wary.

"It's the sun, Mandy. You'll get burned," Sienna explained. "Both of us need hats, as well as sun-screen. The family plot is a good distance away We'll be travelling by car, but we still have to stand in the sun."

"I don't care about the sun," said Amanda. "I've a good mind not to go at all. No one wants me there. *I'm* Mark's widow, yet they're all falling over like ninepins around *you*. It's really weird. Blaine thinks you do it deliberately."

That struck an exposed nerve. "Do what?" Sienna asked shortly.

"Sew people up." Amanda gave an explosive little laugh. "He's right on to you, my girl. I just love your little black dress, by the way. Cute little sleeves. You know, you're very special in your way. And I bet you went out and bought yourself a terrific black hat." She gave a honeyed smirk that really perturbed Sienna.

"Amanda, I shouldn't have to remind you that Mark is being buried today," she told her cousin quietly.

"Come to think of it, Mark *was* a bit suicidal." Amanda sprawled even further down in the armchair, her slender legs outstretched.

Sienna felt her face drain of colour. "He never said such a thing to you, did he?"

"More likely he said it to *you*." Amanda jumped up. "My husband *loved* you, Sienna. He didn't care where he lived as long as it was near you. He was going to dump me for you."

Sienna felt shock allied to very real pain jack-knife through her body. "How many times must I tell you? I was *not* attracted to Mark. Mark was *your* husband."

Amanda looked at her with jaundiced eyes. "He fell in love with you the moment I introduced you."

"Dear God!" Sienna put her hands to her reeling head. "I need to understand this. Mark married *you* when he was in love with *me*?"

"Stranger things have happened, cousin," Amanda drawled. "He used to dream about you."

Sienna whirled about, desperate to get out of the room. "Even if it were true—and it's absolute rubbish—you have to stop this, Amanda. You're determined to hang me for a crime I did not commit."

"You said it. Not me."

Sienna turned back. "You're destroying our relationship, Amanda. Do you realize that?"

"Maybe. But I know what I know." Amanda, for a petite young woman with big blue eyes and a cap of blonde curls, looked as street-tough as they came.

"Then I hope you also know that if you continue to behave badly I'll leave you to fend for yourself. It's high time you did."

Some sense of self-interest clicked inside

Amanda's head. "In that case I *will* behave myself. I'm sorry. I'm just your dumb cousin."

"You're dumb, all right—speaking to Blaine about the money you think you're due." For once Sienna lost control. She was finding it harder and harder to connect with Amanda. "And I consider your telling him *I* put you up to it a real betrayal."

Red flags of colour flew in Amanda's pale cheeks. "He's lying. I told him no such thing. Why would I?"

Sienna made a huge effort to pull herself together. "I'm sorry, Amanda," she said tightly, "but it's the sort of thing that carries your signature. Pulling the rug out from under me is something you consider an achievement. I can't bear to ask what you were trying to get out of Blaine, but if it's way too much you won't get it. Now, I'm going to ask Hilary if she or Marcia have a wide-brimmed hat you could borrow. You don't want to damage your skin. You have such lovely skin."

Amanda brushed away an angry tear. "I can just imagine the sort of hat poor old Hilary could come up with. You might come back with a pith helmet."

"I mightn't come back at all," said Sienna, her hand already on the doorknob.

CHAPTER FIVE

THE graveside service conducted by an Anglican minister was mercifully short. A visibly weak and wilting Amanda stood between Sienna and Blaine, with Hilary, Marcia and other members of the Kilcullen clan to the right of Blaine. A mixed bag. A professor of physics, a federal senator with his wife and daughter, a supreme court judge and his wife, a prominent Kilcullen pastoralist and his family, and another member of the extended Kilcullen family—a wheat and wine grower from somewhere called the Darling Downs.

Sienna later found out it was a wonderfully fertile district on the western slopes of the Great Dividing Range—the mountain barrier than ran down the eastern seaboard and divided the lush coastline from the rolling central plains of Queensland and, beyond, the true Outback.

On the opposite side of the open grave the

mourners were packed. They had come to pay their respects more to the family than poor Mark, Sienna thought, with real sorrow in her heart. She had been experiencing a good deal of torment over Amanda's out-of-the-blue remark that Mark had been suicidal. There *had* been something very worrying about Mark. Now she had to wonder. He had not been an experienced skier, and they had begged Mark to stay on the recognized track, but he had taken off in such a strange way—heading into the trees, one of which had caused his death.

She recalled a moment she had almost forgotten, when Mark had told her he was "worthless" and then immediately laughed it off. Had he really thought himself worthless? If so, why? Having met Mark's family, she couldn't see any one of them working to strip Mark of all self-esteem. Although she could see how it might have felt walking in his half-brother's tall shadow.

Light aircraft had been flying in all morning, causing Amanda to ask irritably, "What is this? An air show? They've been coming in for ages."

"They're Outback families, Mandy. This is a

way of life out here. Don't let it bother you. You have to keep calm."

"Tell me about it!" Amanda said, sounding angry. "I hate this blasted hat."

"Just let me adjust it a little." Sienna tilted the ribbon-decorated, wide-brimmed straw hat further onto Amanda's forehead. "Actually, it looks good on you."

"You can't mean that!" Amanda pushed the hat back again. "I've had to slap sunblock all over my face."

Sienna didn't respond. She was finding it impossible to say the right thing. Amanda would be on show. Everyone would be looking at her, probably judging her. But Sienna thought it more than her life was worth to point that out. Amanda could just as easily decide she wasn't going to the graveside service at all. Amanda was becoming more and more of a mystery as she got older.

The Barrett Family had flown in, in their Cessna, accompanied by their only daughter, Joanne—Joanne who had been Mark's fiancée. Blaine pointed Joanne out very briefly as she and her parents alighted from a station Jeep. An attractive, athletic-looking young woman, sombrely dressed.

A procession of vehicles had been coming and going, ferrying the funeral guests to the Kilcullen family plot set on a low ridge. The area was quite large, surrounded by an arrow-capped, six-foot-high wrought-iron fence painted black. Massive date palms, probably the most ancient cultivated tree in the world, lent some shade, but the chief mourners would be standing directly in the harsh sun.

"That's Joanne, with her mother and father," Blaine told her in a quick aside. "Rachael and Allan Barrett. Amanda doesn't know about Joanne?"

"Not as yet. If I'd told her I don't think I could have got her here."

"Right!" He nodded crisply, leaving her side to speak to another arriving group.

Sienna looked around her quickly, shivering with tension despite the brilliant sunshine. Amanda too was trembling. Amanda had never liked graveyards at the best of time. She had refused point-blank to visit the famous Cimetière du Père-Lachaise when they were in Paris, as though the souls of the writers, artists, poets, composers and other notable figures buried there might rise up and hurt her. Sienna had always found Père-Lachaise a serene place, while Amanda claimed graveyards gave her the creeps.

The true pain was for the living, Sienna thought. Mark's pain was over.

There were too many headstones for an easy count. Blaine and Mark's father lay at rest here. So did Blaine's mother, Marianne. None of the headstones, granite and stone for the most part, could be called in any way a monument—except for one seated marble figure that Sienna assumed was the Kilcullen ancestral figure. Children had been buried there, their graves marked by little guardian angels with spread wings. One showed a small child, a girl with long hair and wearing a dress, lying as if asleep on top of the broad headstone. Sad and touching.

Beside her, Amanda sucked in her breath. "This is too much for me."

Sienna put her arm around her cousin and held her close—if only to muffle her voice. "I know you feel terrible, but we'll get through this together."

* * *

Amanda was perspiring profusely. Heat coloured her very fair skin, and she was stumbling on her feet by the time it was over. Blaine was fully occupied supporting his stepmother, who was grief stricken and not holding up at all. Senator Kilcullen, delegated by Blaine, came swiftly to assist Sienna in getting Amanda back to the waiting Jeep.

"A very difficult time for us all," said the Senator, opening the rear door and gently handing Amanda into the vehicle.

"Thank you, sir." Sienna held out her hand. The Senator took it between both of his, staring in rather a rapt fashion into her face, shaded by the broad brim of her hat. "Sad business, my dear. You're Mark's young widow's cousin, isn't that right?"

"Yes, Senator," she responded gracefully. "Thank you so much.'

"We'll talk more at the house," he promised.

"He won't be talking to *me*," Amanda said behind her hand, all worked up. "I want to be free of all this. I want no grief." The last word was almost spat.

By the time they arrived back at the homestead

a number of people were already gathered in the Great Room. There was to be a buffet lunch for the funeral guests, many of whom had travelled long distances. Hilary herself was stoically receiving people, with a white-faced, unsmiling Marcia standing at her side.

Sienna would have picked Marcia as Mark's twin out of a large crowd. True, the resemblance wasn't as strong as in many other sets of twins, but Marcia was clearly Mark's sister, with the same thick golden brown hair and dark eyes, plus something of his manner. Marcia had been ignoring Amanda—if not pointedly then near enough to it. Sienna was starting to feel very bad about everything.

With good cause.

Amanda was looking around the Great Room aghast. "They needn't think I'm going to be a part of *this*," she said, sweeping the straw hat off her head and throwing it on the nearest chair. Damp blonde curls were stuck in little clusters to her white forehead. "I wouldn't be surprised if I fainted."

"You won't," Sienna said, fearful Amanda might just do that. She really did look ill. Sienna hoped it would be interpreted by the funeral guests as a very natural grief. Amanda *was* the bereaved widow, even if it appeared in private she had moved to a point where the money coming to her was claiming her attention.

The instant Blaine came through the door, physically so impressive, and so much more than that, Sienna knew she had to tell him she had an emergency on her hands.

"What is it, Sienna?"

He broke away from the distinguished, middle-aged couple he'd been escorting into the home-stead to come towards her, staggeringly handsome in funeral clothes relieved by a snowy white shirt. She was aware that beneath the iron control he was feeling his own kind of anguish. The eternal "what might have been".

"I'm sorry, Blaine, but Amanda isn't feeling at all well," she explained quickly. "I'm afraid there are just too many people for her to contend with. I hope you and Hilary won't mind, but I'm taking her upstairs. She's desperate to lie down."

His striking face showed no emotion at all. "Whatever she wants. I could tell she was finding it a tremendous strain. You're coming back again?"

"You want me back?"

"Of course I want you back," he said, as though she had said something out of order.

"Then I'll *be* back. I'll just get Amanda settled."

"Okay," he nodded shortly. "I want you to know I'm giving Amanda enough money to make her secure. So there will be no need for you or your family to offer financial support in the future."

Anger flashed, but she kept her tone level. "Blaine, we've been happy to."

"There's such a thing as being *too* kind," he said tersely, staring down into her upturned face. Like the rest of them she had been standing in full sun, yet she looked as cool as a lily. He had been moved to speak because he had been observing Amanda closely. She had really jumped the gun, questioning him about her legacy. It revealed a decidedly mercenary streak.

On this very day when they had buried Mark he still wasn't sure what had happened that terrible afternoon when their father had suffered his crippling accident. What part had Mark actually played? Mark had been capable of just about anything, Blaine acknowledged, when he was seriously off balance. But he had never been able to speak to anyone of his fears. And his father had lost all memory of the day. Secret fears had to be borne in silence.

By the time Sienna went downstairs again the large crowd of mourners were all but feasting on the lavish buffet lunch, as though any day now they could expect famine. It was no different back home. People seemed to relish a free meal. The buffet had been prepared by Magda and her trained helpers, part-aboriginal girls who worked around the very large homestead. Long mahogany tables were laden with sliced beef fillet, hams, roast pork, pink lamb. There were all kinds of salads, mountains of freshly baked bread rolls. On another table there were bottles and bottles of Scotch, bourbon, red wines and chilled white wines in buckets of ice, frosted glasses.

The mourners were beginning to arrange themselves in little groups. Apart from the family and the Senator, Sienna hadn't met anybody, but gallery work for her father and her own family's position in society gave her an easy self-confidence.

Blaine had been keeping an eye out for her while not appearing to do so. She calmed him in a way he had never experienced with another woman outside his beautiful mother. Burying his half-brother had been a harrowing experience. He deeply regretted their estrangement even if that estrangement, hadn't been of his making, and he mourned Mark, dead so young. The dead didn't age. Only the living could do that.

Just about everyone had offered some comment about Mark's pretty little widow in her blue dress. Most had genuinely found the blue dress touching, others maybe not. He didn't have an opinion himself, although he knew Hilary had been taken aback. All were in agreement, however, about Amanda's stunningly beautiful cousin.

"Prettiness is one thing. Beauty is something entirely different, isn't it?" Joanne had remarked. "I knew straight away which one was Mark's wife. Mark was intimidated by strong, confident women. I'd say the cousin is both."

And a weaver of spells, Blaine thought. She had cast one over Mark. Having met her, he could understand. If he was going to be completely honest she had cast one over him. It brought home to him the powerful reminder that underneath his outward persona he was a sensual man.

Mourners watched in fascination as Sienna made her graceful way to Blaine's side. "Amanda is resting," she said, her eyes moving automatically to his companion.

"Sienna, I'd like you to meet Joanne Barrett." Blaine introduced them. "I've spoken of Joanne."

"Of course. How do you do, Joanne?" Sienna extended her hand, her charming voice gentle and polite. "This is a sad day for you." She could see the flickering disturbance in the young woman's face.

Joanne looked her straight in the eye. "It is indeed. I loved Mark, you know."

Sienna had bargained on hearing this. "Then you must know you have my deepest sympathy, Joanne."

Joanne stood for a moment, as if trying to come to a decision, then said, "Thank you, Sienna. You must meet my parents. Then we should get you something to eat."

"I don't know that I'm hungry," Sienna told her wryly. She was trying to deny her own distress.

"Have something all the same." Blaine realized

Sienna too was striving to keep her feelings at a distance, but he was obliged to turn his head away from her as the Senator called his name, clearly wanting him to join him and his whisky-drinking mates. Drink was always more important than food to those guys, he thought.

"I'll take care of Sienna," Joanne told him, linking her arm through Sienna's. "There's so much I want to know, Sienna. Could you find it in your heart to tell me? I've never been reconciled to Mark's leaving me."

So Joanne hadn't moved on? That was sad. "I'm so sorry, Joanne. I'll tell you what I can, but I never got close to Mark, you know."

"Did anyone?" Joanne asked, grief in her fine hazel eyes. "Did anyone know the *real* Mark?" She choked back tears, sinking her teeth hard into her bottom lip. "He was born to upset people. God forgive me for saying it, today of all days, but everyone here knows about Mark. What happened to the family. What happened to *us*."

"Joanne," Sienna said, very earnestly. "To this day Amanda doesn't know Mark had a fiancée back home."

Joanne's hazel eyes seemed to glaze over. "He never *told* her?"

"He never told anyone. I only found out myself from Blaine when he came to Vancouver. I haven't told Amanda what I know because she's barely holding it all together."

"But what *is* it she's holding together?" Joanne asked in an abruptly cold voice. "I know Amanda is your cousin, and you appear very protective of her, but I don't believe she's the sad and vulnerable little person she makes out to be."

"Why ever would you say that?" Sienna turned on the other woman in surprise, wondering if Blaine had supplied Joanne with only a few facts and left out others. Such as Amanda being ignorant of any fiancée. "Has Blaine said something to you?" She hated the idea of Blaine's discussing her and Amanda with other people, however well-known to him.

Joanne's voice dropped a tone. "Blaine has said very little. It's my friend Marcia who has given us her unsolicited views. Marcy is wound very tight. She had a love-hate going with Mark. Which is to say she was always desperate for a loving brother, but got Mark instead. *Blaine* is her hero figure.

But Blaine is her half-brother. Mark was her *twin*, though he spent most of his time ignoring her."

"I'd say that was Mark's loss, wouldn't you?" Sienna murmured quietly. "How did you come to fall in love with Mark?"

"God knows!" Joanne shrugged. "I didn't ask to. I knew he was cruel, and I can't say he ever made me happy. I knew he was hellishly jealous of Blaine, but he *was* handsome. He could be fun when he was in a good mood. And he was a Kilcullen. Plenty of girls wanted Mark for that reason alone. They knew they couldn't have Blaine."

Sienna found herself asking what she dearly wanted to know. "Does Blaine have someone special?"

Joanne leaned closer. "Blaine could choose a wife from any women he wanted in this room," she said. "See the tall brunette over there, with the great figure? That's Lynda McCrae. Her family run an Outback airline—McCrae Air. Passenger, charter, freight. Blaine and Lynda were an item at one time, but nothing came of it. Not that Lynda isn't still in there trying. Then there's Kerrie Henmann, and I guess Camilla Marsh. All in with a chance. But Blaine lost his father. Blaine worshipped his father. The horrendous accident hit him hard and he had to take over the station, which is a huge job. Mark, of course, took off. That's the sort of person he turned out to be."

Which sadly corresponded to Sienna's own evaluation. "Well, he's laid to rest now, Joanne," she said. "That chapter of your life is closed."

"I hope!" Joanne released a strangled breath. "But I have a funny sort of feeling it isn't. I thought I despised Mark when he took off, but I never wanted him to end his life this way."

"Of course you didn't," Sienna said. "It was a freak accident."

"That's what happened to his father—a freak accident." Joanne paused for a moment, seemingly on the brink of saying more. "My dad didn't like it one bit. Mr Kilcullen was a superb horseman. Dad always says—" She broke off, putting a hand to her mouth.

"Dad says what?" Sienna prompted.

"He wouldn't want me to talk about it." Joanne stared across the Great Room to where her parents were standing talking, plates in hand, to Emily Kilcullen, the Senator's wife. "People couldn't seem to accept what had happened even though accidents happen on stations all the time. We would have known what happened, only Mr Kilcullen lost all memory of that day."

"A terrible thing." Sienna was well able to visualize a strong, powerful man reduced to life in a wheelchair. "People always want to find reasons behind what's happened to those they care about."

"Of course." Joanne sighed. "Dreams don't come true, do they?"

"You're talking about yourself?"

"Yes."

"They won't if you don't reach out, Joanne. There'll be someone for you. I know. But you must put the past aside. You have a future."

Joanne brightened. "How long do you intend to stay, Sienna?"

She could hardly say they'd leave tomorrow if Amanda had her way. "A couple of weeks at least," she replied. "Amanda suffers greatly from jet lag, and we'll be flying the other way—always the worst way to go. So, tell me, what does Marcia have to say about Amanda?"

Joanne moved on, still holding Sienna's arm companionably. "Let's just say Marcy doesn't like her. I hope you can find the time to visit us. Our cattle station, Ettamunga, is only a thirty-minute flight away. It's no Katajangga, of course, but I think you would enjoy the experience. Mum and I would love to hear all about your life, what you do. Blaine said you're an artist. I have to say you look very artistic. I love your accent, by the way. You have the sort of voice that makes a person want to hang onto every word. Ah, there's Mum, waving a hand to us. Let's go over. Say hello. Then I'm going to get you a cold drink and a plate of something. You are just *so* beautiful!" she exclaimed in genuine admiration. "But I guess you're used to hearing that. Why aren't *you* married? Blaine said you weren't."

So Blaine had volunteered that piece of information. "Hey, now, I'm not drawing my pension yet." She smiled.

Sienna caught Blaine's eye across the room. It struck her as she met his gaze that she had been missing something crucial in her life. Blessed with youth, health, inherited good-looks and her gift as an artist, with a mother, father and brother she adored, there was still that *empty* spot needing to be filled. By a man, by a soulmate. Her loyalty to Amanda remained intact, but she had to face the fact that if Amanda were not her cousin she would never have chosen her for a friend. They were just too different, and becoming even more so.

She had never been short of men friends, when it came to that. She'd had two fairly serious affairs and had considered marriage, but in the end backed off. Why? Both men would have made good husbands and fathers, but in the end she'd had to confront the fact she hadn't *loved* them. Or not enough. She wanted a man to *fill* her up. Fill up her life. She wanted a man she could be passionate about—a man who would be passionate about her. She wanted that *soul mate* she had been beginning to think would never come along. Maybe she was too choosy. But she wanted *total* love.

And into her life had come Blaine Kilcullen. *Beware of what you wish for.*

It was mid-afternoon before the private planes, the charter planes and the fleets of four-wheel drive vehicles left for their journey home. A broken-hearted Hilary had retired to her room, the immense struggle to hold back her grief no longer necessary, and Joanne had taken charge of her friend Marcia. Marcia had gone to stay with the Barretts for a day or two. Everyone knew of Hilary's love for her wayward son. They knew Mark, for all his difficult nature, had been the favourite twin. Sienna had the feeling Marcia had gone off so easily because of that factor, and no doubt to escape Amanda.

In her room, Sienna changed into a tangerine cotton shirt, tucking it into a pair of cream cotton twill pants, and slipping on sneakers. She didn't quite know what to do with herself. She thought she might ask Magda if there was anything she could do to help, although Magda and her girls had already made inroads into the big job of clearing away. Still, she would ask. If Magda refused help she would take a walk around the rear gardens. But first she had to call in on Amanda.

"Well, *you're* late!" Amanda was sprawled atop the four-poster bed, wearing a silk caftan.

"Excuse me?"

Amanda was inspecting her wristwatch for all the world like an employer clocking a recalcitrant employee. "It's half past three."

"Pity you couldn't have made it downstairs, if only for a half-hour," Sienna retorted. "People really wanted to meet you."

"Oh, yeah!" Amanda snorted. "They were looking at me like I was some sort of a freak. And that Marcia! She hates me."

"She doesn't. But you haven't been particularly nice to her. Anyway, she's gone back with the Barrett family. The daughter, Joanne, is a close friend."

"God, I didn't know she had one. Anyway, that's your job, isn't it? Winning people over."

"Joanne was Mark's fiancée at one time." Might as well get it over. At least Amanda was lying down.

"I knew he had one," Amanda said, casually admitting a long deception.

"And you never said a word?" Sienna was aghast.

"What was it to *you*?" Amanda asked querulously. "Mark said she'd been mad about him since they were kids. His mother more or less forced him into the engagement, but he couldn't hack it."

"He couldn't hack marriage either, could he?" Sienna said with a rush of anger.

"God, you're not going to make a scene, are you?" Amanda half sat up, looking like an innocent under unfair attack. "Can't you see I'm sick?"

Sienna backed off. The habit was ingrained. "I *can* see, Amanda. But you'd feel better if you'd been getting some food into you these past days. You've lost weight and you can't afford to. You're starting to look like a waif."

"That's it! Rub it in." Amanda fell back to thrash the pillows. "Mark and I might have been heading for disaster, but I loved him."

"Some part of you may have. But you wanted Mark, right or wrong. You have to take some responsibility for that."

Amanda's milky white cheeks blotched. "Thanks for your compassion. I'd like to go home, only I don't think I can face the long trip yet. I might go to Sydney. I liked the look of Sydney. I might go when I feel better and Blaine hands over the money."

"The money, the money! Was the sole reason for your coming here the money?"

"You bet!" Amanda gave her a droll look.

"Then I'd strongly advise you to allow Blaine to choose the time," Sienna warned her.

Amanda stretched her slender arms above her hand. "Then I won't have to run to you and Lucien any more."

Sienna stared at her cousin in dismay. She had spent most of her life looking out for "little Mandy". Her parents had been endlessly supportive. Apparently it all counted for nothing with Amanda. "Is that all we've meant to you, Amanda?" she asked sadly.

Amanda laughed. "God, no! Just joking. I love you to bits. But please don't sermonize, Sienna. I've had enough of it."

"Okay." Sienna turned about. "Is there anything I can get you?' Amanda really did look sickly. She wondered if she had a bottle of something secreted in her room.

"A pitcher of martinis?" Amanda suggested.

"Cup of tea and a sandwich? Magda is pretty flat out, but I can get it for you."

"Don't bother," said Amanda. "I'll have something sent up later."

* * *

Magda had allowed Sienna to take charge of the crystal glasses. Although coasters had been placed strategically around the Great Room, both she and Magda had paused to cluck over a couple of rings on the gleaming timber surfaces.

"People are so careless." Magda had shaken her heavy blonde head. "Not to worry, Sienna. I have a good trick for removing marks."

Now Sienna was in the kitchen, a huge room with "Magda's Domain" on a brass plaque fixed to the door, accessible from the corridor adjacent to the left staircase. They were talking easily— Magda telling Sienna her story of how as a young Polish migrant she had been taken in by the Kilcullens when her Lithuanian partner had left her penniless and stranded in Darwin.

Magda broke off as Blaine walked in. He was dressed pretty much as Sienna was, in shirt and jeans, only he wore riding boots that made him even taller.

"I've been looking for you, Sienna," he said, sending his sizzling glance in her direction. He crossed to where Magda was standing, placing a hand on her comfortably padded shoulder. "Thank you, Magda," he said quietly.

Magda coloured up. "I do anything for you, Mr Blaine," she said. "You want to take this beautiful young lady off?"

"Got it in one. I need to get out of the house," Blaine said, the strain of the day showing on his dynamic face. "I thought you would too, Sienna. You ride?"

"I'm a Canadian, aren't I?" she said with a lift of her brows.

"Thank God for that. I knew you would. There can't be anyone in the world who hasn't heard of the Royal Canadian Mounties and the Calgary Stampede. Horse-riding must be something of a passion in Canada, just like here. I thought we'd take same horses."

"You go now, Sienna."

Magda waved Sienna off—as though she needed any encouragement. The atmosphere at the homestead had become almost unbearably claustrophobic.

Blaine let her take her pick of mounts, bar his own—a stunning sooty bay called Amir. Its gleaming coat was almost completely black, but it had a bay's points, black mane, tail and legs.

"It looks a temperamental animal," she said,

eyeing the big gelding. It was dancing skittishly, and Blaine was taking a moment or two to control him. It couldn't have been plainer that Amir was raring to go.

"Just what I like."

Blaine glanced across at her with taut approval. Her every movement was so fluid she might have been buoyed by the breeze. She was wearing a cream akubra he had taken from the station store. It was not only a perfect fit, it suited her to perfection. She had secured her long hair in a thick, glowing plait. He was grateful her flawless skin wasn't the milky, very sensitive kind of the redhead that threw up freckles for protection. It was a load off his mind. Amanda's skin was much thinner and whiter, which could be a real problem in the desert sun, but Sienna's was creamy, and didn't burn given adequate protection. In fact she had already taken on a little colour. She'd had the foresight to pack gleaming riding boots, so she had fully expected to ride. It pleased him greatly that she shared his love of horses. He could feel his blood rising—as though *nothing*, not even the grief of Mark's funeral, could snuff out the sexual excitement she engendered.

"So, handsome horses for handsome people," she was saying, throwing him a half-smile over her shoulder. "I think I'll have this one, if I may." She stopped at a stall where a beautiful bright chestnut mare with a white star on its forehead was definitely looking for her attention. The mare clearly liked her, nuzzling her ear while she tickled its neck.

"Tamara. Good choice," Blaine clipped out. "Especially when we plan on galloping to the horizon." His expression was that of a man who needed to get moving. If only away from temptation.

The going ahead looked fast and fair. They rode at full gallop the minute they came to the open plains country, giving the eager horses their heads. Big, sturdy-legged gelding and smaller white-socked mare rose to the challenge. It was impossible to avoid the paper daisies. No help for it! They carpeted the landscape! So the horses' hooves cut wide swathes through their glory. To Sienna it was a tremendous relief, like coming out of a sick stupor.

When they eventually slowed Sienna fancied Blaine's smouldering expression had lightened.

"You're good." He gave his verdict the minute she brought the fleet chestnut mare alongside the taller, stronger gelding.

"Know why? I've been riding since I was a child. Just like you. I love it."

"It shows."

"So nice to have your approval."

It was a mocking little thrust, he acknowledged.

Gusts of heady scent from a patch of velvety red wild flowers were being drawn into her lungs. The perfume was so sweetly, exotically overpowering Sienna thought it could easily make her woozy if she was exposed to it long enough.

"How different the landscape is to my own British Columbia," she mused. They had moved off, heading towards water.

"Well, it *would* be," he said dryly. "Isn't British Columbia renowned for its beautiful verdant landscapes, powerful rivers, forests, lakes, snow-capped mountains?"

She nodded with pride, adjusting her thick plait. "This is another world. It speaks a different language. The language of your indigenous people. This landscape is unique to anything I've ever seen, and I've seen a lot of really fabulous desert country in the US. This is the red planet Mars, only it's covered in wild flowers mile after mile."

"You couldn't get used to it?"

Now, why the hell had he asked that? But mercifully, she didn't appear to attach much significance to his question so far as he could see.

"Oh, *yes!*" she exclaimed. "My imagination is fired to the extent I'm storing away scenes for the future. I can paint from photographs if I have to. There's wonderful inspiration here for an artist. The pervading sense of antiquity must be one of the Outback's greatest attractions. That and its mystique: the lonely wilderness, the extreme isolation, those extraordinary rocks. It's dramatic and lyrical at the same time. And the *colours!* All the dry pigment powders—yellow ochre, Venetian red, burnt umber, raw umber, burnt sienna, bright yellow, the blacks and the flake whites. Incredible. That flat-topped mesa way off in the distance appears a deep violet, and even that tree is simply beautiful, framed by the blue sky."

"Ghost gum." He identified the lovely Outback species, feeling his link to her strengthen by the minute.

"Of course—with that stark white bole. Some

great being from your Dreamtime must have scattered those boulders about."

They were heading towards a broad glittering expanse of water, visible through the thick screen of trees. Bright golden spears of desert Spinifex grew in clumps here, circling the ferrous red boulders, big and small, that were scattered over the desert sands at random.

"Devil's marbles." Blaine's silver-grey eyes were steady on her profile as he asked a question. "Are you glad you came along?"

"What, now? Or for the trip?"

"Both."

She took a deep breath. There had been so many emotions unlocked inside her. Emotions she hadn't even known she was capable of. "I wouldn't have missed it for the world."

It was the absolute truth.

Blaine's face grew still. "Then I guess we owe thanks to Mark for that. I suppose there's a hidden purpose in everything?"

"I'm sure there is."

Sienna faced it squarely. If she longed for high romance she had a feeling she was going to get it—if only briefly. They lived in vastly different worlds, separated by a great ocean. But her rising attachment to Blaine Kilcullen, however well she was managing to hide it, was starting to seriously implode on her life. She couldn't be in his presence without her whole body quickening. She couldn't even *think* of him without experiencing shooting thrills. She had come to believe she was a woman in control of her life. She now found she was as vulnerable as the next woman. Falling in love was like being set adrift from one's moorings. Her feelings that were running so strongly seemed quite separate from herself. Or the self she had thought she was. The truth was she was being swept away.

In the wrong place, at the wrong time.

CHAPTER SIX

SIENNA hadn't been expecting to come upon such a very large body of water, covering she estimated at least five acres. It was more like a wetlands, with huge pink water lilies and aquatic plants and grasses massed thickly around the water's edge. The water lilies held their exquisite faces up out of a great lake that looked as if it would be quite deep at the centre. It came to a dead end to the left, and to the right the broad stretch of water narrowed into a channel that disappeared around a tree-lined bend.

The water had taken its colour from the densely blue sky. Overhanging trees preened in their own reflection. The surface was still and crystal-clear.

They had tethered the horses, were walking together in silence down to the pale yellow sand. The air was remarkably pure. Birds warbled in colonies from the trees, or flitted from one side of the bank to the other, their brilliant plumage glistening like jewels in the sun. She had been fascinated by the great flocks of tiny green and yellow birds, the budgerigar of the wild, that had followed them on their ride. Once Blaine had called a halt so she could admire the perfectly co-ordinated flight displays they were turning on, involving swift twists and turns, always in an impressive arrowhead formation.

"I somehow had the idea a billabong was just a pool," she remarked. "This is a very large sheet of water." She took off her akubra and threw it so deftly it landed on a flat topped boulder nearby. On impulse she pulled off the covered elastic band that held her plait, shaking her hair free. "Ah, that's better!"

Watching her, Blaine felt a great thrust of desire. Cupid's arrow through the heart, he thought grimly. Her long, magnificent silky mane flew back in the air like some darn TV commercial. He wanted to reach out and take a great swathe of it in his hand, wrap it around his wrist, draw her into him.

She turned back. Aware? Unaware? A woman like that would be able to read men with ease. He removed his wide-brimmed hat, aiming it unerringly so it landed beside hers.

"Billabong is an aboriginal word, most probably from the Wiradjuri." His voice showed no hint of his inner turbulence. "In the early days claims were put forward that billabong was of Scottish Gaelic origin. Who knows? Nearly all our early settlers, especially Outback pioneers, hailed from the British Isles anyway. But I go with the aboriginal. You might know the most famous reference to a billabong—in the opening lines of Banjo Paterson's 'Waltzing Matilda'. It nearly became our National Anthem way back in 1974, only 'Advance Australia Fair' beat it to it."

"So sing it for me," she teased gently. "Try out your voice." He had a very attractive speaking voice, dark and resonant, not dusky-mellow, but very crisp and clean.

"As it turns out, I'm game to sing you the opening lines," he said. "That's if you're not trying to take a rise out of me—which I suspect you are. People in the Outback are fiercely proud of 'Matilda'."

"Okay." She nodded at him approvingly "Let's hear it." He would be a baritone, for sure.

She didn't quite know what she would hear, but found she was swept by a rush of pleasure as he began to sing to her. When she had first met him she had thought him very much on the severe side, even daunting, but plainly he had his lighter moments.

He started off quietly, warmly, with innate musicality. A simple song, yet his rendering of it stunned her. She felt a lump in her throat, the sting of tears at the back of her eyes. Lord knew how she would react if he broke into a love song.

"How's that?" he asked when he was finished, his silver eyes sparkling with provocation.

The moment had turned from a bit of fun into something extraordinarily intimate. "Wonderful!" she said, clapping her hands and thus disturbing birds that shrieked instant protest.

"Great! So what do we do *now*?" he asked very coolly.

The question, allied to the look in his brilliant eyes, threw her completely off guard. "Well, I know what *I'm* going to do," she said after a moment, making a huge effort to quell the excitement he was deliberately creating. "I'm going to splash my face with water."

Cool down. That's the girl! In no time at all you'll be going home.

"Go for it!" he said, his voice now openly taunting.

She chose a spot where clear water pooled in the depression around a big boulder that was half in and half out of the water. Bending, she scooped up handfuls. "Ooh!" She had no idea the water would be so *cold*! But she continued, splashing her face and neck several times. It was so refreshing. The water spilled down over her shirt and ran in a channel between her breasts. She turned to face him.

Her golden sherry eyes were shimmering, her skin radiant, her beautiful hair luxuriously tangled. He was filled with the fierce need to hold her. He had never dreamed of anything like this. He certainly hadn't planned it.

"Want to take a picture of me?" She was only joking, but the expression on his handsome face stopped her. "Blaine?"

"I don't have a camera right now."

He was walking towards her, the most exciting, magnetic man in the world. Close to, he brushed back a stray curl. "You're a very beautiful woman," he said, in a dark brooding voice.

Her reply was tense and guarded. "Sometimes I'm not sure that's a good thing."

"Meaning what?" He stared down into her eyes. He was holding himself tightly in check when the very closeness of her was electrifying him.

"What do *you* think I mean?" she retorted with spirit. "I know you have trouble trying to fit me into the scheme of things."

He nodded. "I can't deny I want to know the answer to one question. Did you have an affair with Mark?"

All of a sudden she felt as if she was suffocating. "Damn you, Blaine." She went to stalk past him only he caught her back, one arm encircling her waist. She was at once inflamed and chilled. "I find you absolutely *hateful*!" she cried.

"Except your body is telling me something very different."

Powerful emotions were rising like a sea creature from the great ocean depths. "This isn't right, Blaine." The moan that issued from her throat was low and plaintive.

"I know."

The trembling in her body had to be betraying her. She was so close to him she could feel his breath on her hair. "Attraction—mutual attraction—is a funny thing, isn't it?" he pondered. "*Elemental*. You try to fight it but it makes no difference. You're powerless." As he spoke he was pulling her in tight to his lean body, compounding the sizzling sexual tension.

She should have been offering resistance—except one of her hands, as if it had a life of its own, was clutching at the front of his shirt and holding tight. Attraction wasn't just elemental, it was *merciless*.

When his mouth came down hard and deep on hers it was such shattering excitement that, the need that pulsed between them was heightened by a tiny element of violence. It was as though both were at war with the force that had so fiercely and easily overtaken them. When his hand shaped, then cupped her breast, his thumb working the taut, aroused nipple, her mind and body went into a spin. Desire was like a fever coming on her, making her light-headed. He was whispering something into her open mouth, but she couldn't make out the words she was so far gone. She had thought she longed for an overwhelming passion, but passion at this level was a snare. It could destroy her and her ordered life. If he didn't stop kissing her and caressing her she thought she might just offer herself to him like some sort of sacrifice.

When Blaine jerked back his dark head, his voice reflected immense strain. "I needed to do that," he rasped. "I've done it."

"Like it was on your 'Before-I-die' list? You've done what you intended to do all along?" she gasped, her thoughts chaotic. "Is it going to be dangerous to be alone with you? Is that it?" She was angered now, such was the ambivalence of human nature and the ways of woman with man.

The vertical line between his black brows looked ominous. "You *know* there's something very powerful between us, Sienna. It couldn't be plainer. So don't for the love of God pretend you don't."

The sternness of his voice set her teeth on edge. To her horror, she found herself reacting blindly. She struck out with her fist, hitting the hard wall of his chest. "I know *nothing* can come of it," she cried in frustration, and then abruptly all anger drained out of her. She didn't even know how to go on. The strength of her passions had thrown her completely off balance. "I'm sorry— I'm sorry," she apologized. "I shouldn't have hit you. I've never done such a thing in my life. But you make me so *mad*. Lord knows, I've never attacked a man before."

"And it has you shaking." He put steadying hands on her shoulders.

The concern in his voice actually stoked the dying flame. "Ever heard of a romantic nightmare?" she challenged. She had been referring to the situation between *them*—only Amanda's claim that Mark had dreamt of her shot like an arrow into her mind.

"Give it to me straight, Sienna," Blaine said determinedly. "Were you and Mark having an affair that ultimately *you* wanted to break off?"

Her eyes looked enormous in her over-wrought face. "I'm sorry, Blaine. I don't want to get into this. And I won't accept your efforts to try and allot blame to me. You're in no position to judge."

"How can I judge what I don't know?" he retaliated. "You don't think you might at least offer me the truth? What *did* happen? Something did.

I'm not a fool. My every instinct tells me Mark was madly in love with *you*. Not his wife, your cousin. *You!*"

She went limp, in need of comfort. "We buried him today, Blaine. He had so little time."

"Do you think I've forgotten that?" His strong hands clenched on her shoulders.

"You're hurting me," she said after a moment. It was awful to fight with him.

"I'm sorry." He released her immediately, but his expression remained tormented. "I don't seem to be able to think of anything else. All these secrets—things kept hidden, held back."

"That happens in every family, I should think," she offered in a toneless voice.

"Far too much of it in my family," he said, his expression bleak. "We might as well ride back now."

Sienna said nothing. She replaited her hair, then reached for her hat. Some part of her desperately wanted to tell him of that ghastly late afternoon when his half brother had tried his hardest to force a sexual response from her. Only even now she felt shamed. To tell him she would be forced to tell him *everything*, to reveal the darkness at

Mark's core. What good would come of that? Her conscience was clear. She'd been innocent of any wrongdoing then. She was innocent now.

Yet the shade of Mark was still around to threaten her.

Dusk had fallen before they arrived back at the homestead. Blaine headed towards the west wing, his own private retreat. Sienna pulled herself up the timber staircase, reluctant to call in on Amanda for fear of what she might find. Amanda had well and truly turned to alcohol for comfort. There was the possibility she could be lying in bed drunk. God Forbid. All the devotion Amanda had been offered through the years. Had it ever counted?

Blaine would most probably be speaking to her in the morning about her legacy. Amanda had better make sure she made a better impression than she had been making so far.

With a feeling she was shocked to recognise as dread, she knocked on Amanda's door, hearing with relief Amanda's voice call clearly, "Come in."

Amanda's blue eyes swept her cousin's willowy frame, down to her riding boots.

"So where have *you* been?" she asked archly.

"Out for a ride."

"Alone?"

"Of course not. Blaine was with me. This is the most extraordinary place. You should see it."

"Don't really want to, sweetie. The desert ain't my thing. Course, Blaine could be—but he's not interested in me, is he?" There was something terribly suggestive in the way Amanda posed the question.

"Ah, give me a break!" Sienna said. "Blaine has just lost his brother."

"*Half*-brother," Amanda corrected. "No two men could be less alike."

Sienna turned away. "Are you coming down to dinner? I think you should."

"No way!" Amanda shook her head. "Do you reckon Mark could have had anything to do with his dad's accident?" she asked as Sienna was almost at the door.

"What?" Sienna was so stunned she stopped in her tracks. "What are you saying?"

"And you're supposed to be the genius?" Amanda vented her jealousy. "Don't you think it was odd the way Mark got stuck into his family, particularly Blaine, but he couldn't be drawn much on his father. No-go territory. I used to get the feeling Mark was guilty of some stupidity, some rash act. You know how he used to go off half-cocked. Maybe he caused his father's accident. Didn't mean to—but that was Mark. Damn it, Sienna, he sort of killed *himself*, didn't he?"

Sienna felt a vibration along her spine. "We'll never know."

"Another one of those great mysteries!" Amanda declared.

"I know Mark carried a great burden," Sienna said. "But there's no use thinking about it. Mark is no longer with us."

"And he never got to have the woman he had the hots for."

"I don't know you at all, do I?" Sienna was labouring to keep calm. "Have you lost *all* feeling for Mark?"

"You have no idea how *hard* it was for me." Amanda's blue eyes flashed. "He'd have sex with me, pretending it was *you*.'

Sienna grasped the porcelain doorknob, desperate to get out of the room. "Do you know how terrible you sound? Please be on your best behaviour tomorrow. That's probably when Blaine will want to talk to you. I know how good you are at play-acting, so try to remember you're Mark's grieving widow."

"Ain't that the truth?" Amanda lifted her blonde head, then slammed it back into the pillows. "Tell the housekeeper I'd like a light chicken dish for dinner. Some white wine. Maybe a scoop of vanilla ice cream for dessert. I'm not keeping things down, I'm so out of whack. Why did you ever persuade me to come here, Sienna?" she wailed, for all the world like a child.

"I didn't persuade you, Amanda," Sienna felt eerily calm. "You came because you thought there was a good deal of money in it for you."

"Afraid for once I'll have more than you?"

"Anything to make you happy," Sienna said, facing for perhaps the first time in her life that deep in her heart Amanda hated her. It stung her like the bite of a hidden viper.

Just the two of them for dinner. Hilary's doctor had given her a knock-out pill, and Marcia had contacted the homestead to say they had arrived safely on Ettamunga. She would stay overnight with Joanne and her family.

"Mum doesn't need me," she had lamented, and for a moment Blaine hadn't known what to say—because there was more than a grain of truth in that. "I could see it in her eyes. She wants to mourn Mark on her own. She has never faced the truth about him. She never will. He was her son. Her daughter got left out in the cold. I don't know what I would do, Blaine, if it wasn't for you."

It was at that point he'd made a decision. Marcia needed help right away. He would send her to stay with the Senator and his wife in Sydney. They would happily take her in. If she liked it in Sydney he would buy her an apartment, with family close by. Marcia had enjoyed an excellent education. Time for her to get on with her life.

He would have to find another solution for Hilary. Not her own family. They had never wanted Hilary, had been amazed and overjoyed to see her taken off their hands by his father. His expression grew sombre as he considered Hilary hadn't had much of a life. But then like Marcia she hadn't taken life on. One had to.

Neither of them was hungry. Magda, knowing

this, served a platter of thickly sliced ham with a bowl of salad Niçoise. They shared a bottle of red. It was more than enough. Both skipped dessert, settling for coffee. But because she had baked them fresh, Magda couldn't resist piling several of her peanut butter cookies on a plate.

They moved to the seating arrangement in front of a great stone fireplace. "Do you mean to speak to Amanda tomorrow?" Sienna asked after a while.

Blaine picked up one of the cookies and took a bite. "You mean about the money?" His brilliant eyes lighted on her.

"You know I mean about the money."

"Not the first time it's been brought to my attention," he said dryly.

"Thank God *I* have no interest in your money, Blaine. I have a life of my own. I'm successful, and I intend to become even more so."

"I haven't the slightest doubt you will," he said, with outward suavity and an inner sense of coming deprivation. "Have you ever wondered if your cousin deserves your devotion?"

She set her coffee cup down. "You don't like her, do you?"

His eyes on her were piercingly intent. "At this point I'm wondering what's to like? I realize Amanda is heavily jet lagged—we've all made allowances for that—but she's shown no spark of kindness towards Hilary and Marcia. She's ignored them in their own home. They really were prepared to welcome her. They've had no difficulty taking to *you*. You have great people skills."

"Maybe it's because I *like* people," she returned. "Although I have reason to make an exception of you."

"Ah, don't be like that, Sienna," he mocked darkly.

"Just so you know."

"You have a circle of golden light around your head," he said, studying the effect. "*Are* you an angel?"

She ignored him. She knew he was baiting her. "The chandeliers?" she queried. "It's a superb collection. I've been meaning to ask you who started it."

"Who started it?" He repeated the question, rather forlornly for such a dynamic man. "My dad. He imported the lot of them some time after my mother died. I've grown up with them. Some people think they're completely over the top. I suppose they are."

"Well, I love them," she said, staring up at the great gilt, bronze and crystal chandelier above their heads. "They add a touch of fantasy—magic, if you like. They must be very valuable. They're all antique."

He nodded. "The one over us is Russian—circa 1840. I guess my father's aim was to *light up* the homestead. He wanted to bring brilliance and luminosity back when he thought he had lost it for ever. The light must have reminded him of my mother in some way."

"I can understand that," Sienna said quietly, surprised by the sting of tears in her eyes. "Where *is* the portrait of your mother? You told me it has never been taken down. I would dearly love to see it."

"And you shall, Cinderella. It used to hang in pride of place at the top of the gallery, but after Dad died I changed things around. The west wing had always been mine, but for some reason I can't quite explain I shifted back into the main house—the old master suite. Hilary had chosen elsewhere after their marriage. I had the portrait removed to the west wing. Finish your coffee and I'll take you."

"Will you step into my parlour?" said the spider to the fly.

"Will you, won't you, will you, won't you, will you join the dance?"

Sienna walked with him quite calmly, but as usual she was anything but calm. Her heart was beating faster with every step, her head crammed with snapshots of their afternoon together—that fierce, deeply passionate kiss. Was it really possible to fall hopelessly in love at a single glance?

She feared the answer was *yes.*

The west wing, bigger than the average house, was exactly *him*: dynamic, exciting, full of surprises. He wasn't just a cattle baron, he was a man of culture. She had realized that from the very beginning.

"Wow!" she exclaimed as she looked at the carved panels—leaves, flowers, fruits, animals— obviously Asian, that surrounded his front door.

"Balinese screens," he said. "I had them cut to fit. Come on in."

"I'd love to. How we decorate our private sanctuaries says a lot about us. Now I can find out more about you."

"Are you sure you want to?"

Her hands trembled, so she linked them behind her back. Unlike in the main house there was a foyer, with a big carved chest with a bronze head on it, a large painting in a heavy gilded frame above it, and a glorious Iranian rug with fiery tones. But what dazzled her eye was the magnificent painting on the facing wall.

"Wherever did you get this?" She moved across the rug to examine the large canvas with a professional eye.

"On a trip to Rome," he said, standing back, the better to observe her. "It's seventeenth century, but unsigned. Even so, it cost an arm and leg."

"I'm not surprised. It's so powerful! Probably the work of a very good apprentice who studied under a leading painter of the time. Clearly your artist was influenced by Rubens. Those are Rubenesque horses. Just look at the long, flowing, curling manes and tails. I've seen a horse like this in the Prado in Madrid. A Spanish grandee astride a white horse. Only these two rearing beauties are doing battle. It's savage in its way, isn't it?"

Very gently she touched the surface of the aged canvas. The horses' coats had a wonderful satiny-pearlescent lustre. The background was a rich orange-red, with broad strokes of gold, a palette that Blaine had picked up with the Persian rug.

"What more treasures do you have for me?"

"A lot of aboriginal paintings," he said. "I collect the best of them. We have some very fine indigenous artists." He led the way off to the right of the central panel, obviously specially constructed to take the painting. "This is the living room. The dining room on the other side. As you can see, I favour our region's colours."

Sienna looked around the very generous space with a rush of pleasure. In some ways it reminded her of a house her father once rented in Marrakech: the strong contrast between white walls and the fiery red-orange-ochre elements. Another splendid Iranian rug in rich tones, with a large ornately carved coffee table atop it, divided two bronze leather sofas with dark red damask scatter cushions. Two deep armchairs were covered in cream leather. One entire was given over to a built-in mahogany bookcase filled with books. There were paintings galore.

"Have you ever been to Marrakech?" she asked.

"I've been most everywhere—including the South Pole," he said. "I have yet to explore beautiful Canada, but I will when I get the time."

"I hope so." Her eyes were on an exotic looking planter's chair made of cane, and a bamboo and lacquer octagonal small table nearby.

"Time enough to look around," he said. "You wanted to see the portrait of my mother? It's in my study. Pride of place. As you can imagine, a bravura painting of a beautiful woman demands its own space. Besides, it wouldn't fit in with all the other paintings. Come along."

"Of course! You're my guide."

He turned back so suddenly she almost slammed into him. "So what are you going to do to pay for your tour?"

The blood started to pound in her ears. He looked extremely handsome and a little daunting "I don't know. What about telling you how clever you are?"

"It will do for a start."

More timber panelling, this time in light golden

tones, and a big, very workmanlike desk—masculine design. Midnight-blue leather sofas were grouped around a big square glass-topped table with a very interesting sculpture of an Indian goddess on it. But, as he had said, in pride of place behind his desk was a large portrait of a very beautiful dark-haired, magnolia-skinned woman with the silver-grey eyes she had passed on to her son. She was wearing an exquisite white duchesse satin gown with a silvery sheen. Around her throat hung an opera-length string of large pearls. Diamond earrings with pearl drops fell from her ears. She was sitting in a high backed gilded chair; the background was a muted deep blue.

"She looks quite unforgettable," Sienna said, thinking her father would love to see this portrait and give his private opinion of it.

"Doesn't she? That's her wedding gown."

"It's beautiful. Now I know where you get your extraordinary eyes from. Do you remember her?"

"I remember some things," he said, in a dark sombre tone. "I remember when she died. It was the only time I ever saw my father cry. Grief just burst out of him. He couldn't hold it back. He never got over her."

"It must have been a great tragedy—for you and him."

His eyes remained fixed on the portrait. "My mother's life ended too soon. Now Mark's. Dad married Hilary to give me a surrogate mother. It some ways it might have been the worst thing he ever did.'

Her heart was wrung for Hilary. "But, Blaine, Hilary had their children—the twins."

"I think that was the closest my stepmother got to real happiness," he brooded. "At least for a few years. Dad couldn't have been kinder or more considerate to Hilary. She had everything she wanted. But she always knew he didn't love her."

"She must have known that before he married her?" Sienna reasoned.

"Of course."

"Well, then, it was her decision. She may have got more out of her marriage than you think."

"I'd like to think so, Sienna." He sighed. "I'm fond of Hilary, only it didn't work out. Mark was difficult right from the start. Marcia too. But, being a girl, very much less so. Dad always said he recognized Hilary's family in the twins. The only good thing Hilary ever did as far as her family was concerned was to get my father to marry her."

A look of sad acceptance settled on Sienna's face. "We can't pick our parents, but we can make our own lives, Blaine.'

"Not so easy when one inherits a problematic temperament. It's all in the genes. One should really think about that before getting married."

She turned to him. "So, are you moving on that? Getting married? Joanne pointed out a trio of likely candidates to me."

"Everyone wants to marry me off," he said. "Including Joanne. I have to tell you I've no urge to walk down the aisle right now."

"Well, men like you are obliged to obey the rules. You know—provide heirs. You have a great deal to hand on."

He pinned her gaze. "You're trying to get under my skin, aren't you?"

"Is that possible?"

"Back off, Sienna," he warned.

There was a faintly taunting edge to her voice.

"Hey, who has the problem now?" She turned to the door, a willowy figure in her short summery dress printed with yellow and red poppies gone wild. "I love the portrait of your most beautiful mother, but now show me the rest of your domain. It's so very *you*. Why did you ever leave it?"

"Sentiment, I suppose," he said, following her out.

"I thought you might be rather short on that." She spoke with feigned casualness, but the fact was she was deliberately provoking him. Where was the sense in that?

Back off. Back off. He told you to.

The dining room setting was for eight—six Spanish-style chairs and two carvers surrounding a polished timber table. The walls were orange, with two very powerful aboriginal paintings to either side of the French doors that led out onto the grounds. Each painting depicted a different version of an orange-scarlet sunset reflected in the waters of a billabong surrounded by mounds of golden Spinifex, with a low flat-topped mesa in cobalt blue in the background. On the wall above the sideboard hung a long indigenous painting of the Central Desert region, with its rolling fiery red sand hills.

"A woman of the Eastern Arrente people," he told her, seeing her interest. "Self-taught."

"She's wonderful. I could sell paintings like these back home in less than a minute. I could never capture this particular vision—this passion for the land of birth, the intimacy with an incredible landscape and its land forms, the unique way of expressing that passion on canvas."

"The land is everything to aboriginal culture," Blaine said. "Many of our indigenous artists have been taught by white people, but they paint in their own way—not ours."

"That's all to the good."

"I think so. The kitchen leads off here," he said. "When my polo pals fly in for a casual game I entertain them here."

"You do the cooking?" It wouldn't have surprised her if he had said yes.

"Sienna, we have an excellent cook in the house," he pointed out dryly. "Magda does the cooking and the serving. She would be greatly offended if I didn't leave it to her."

"That's the way women are with heroes." Sienna

sighed. "'I'm here for you. Just tell me what I can do.'"

His eyes glittered like diamonds. "I caught that note of derision, Sienna."

She looked back at him in feigned astonishment. "I'm sorry, Blaine. I didn't mean anything. I'm being utterly sincere."

"I think you're forgetting I have a devil in me."

"And I don't have the slightest desire to raise him."

There was a stone fireplace in the bedroom—"Desert nights in the Dry can be very cold," he said—and another stunning aboriginal painting, this time with a palette of blues and featuring birds in flight. The huge bed was custom-made, with a carved bedhead and carved side tables. Indonesian, Blaine said. A magnificent carved chest at the foot of the bed held a mix of exotic objects—a Cambodian Buddha head covered in silver leaf in particular—no doubt from his travels.

"For a cattleman you have a great sense of theatre," she said, more fascinated with every passing second.

"I like to use what I collect. Dressing room. Master bath. Want to take a look?"

"Sure. When do you get to wear these suits?" she asked, admiring the rows of tailored suits, the high-quality cabinetry, the shelves holding dress shirts on one side, bush shirts and casual shirts on the other.

"I do have another life," he said dryly. "Katajangga the working cattle station is nowadays only a small part of our family interests. We have substantial mining interests, real estate, vineyards. My grandfather had the great good sense to realize we had to diversify."

"So you get to the cities often?"

"I do. I have a great overseer, which makes things easier for me. You'll meet him when things settle down a little. Zack Mangan. He has a wife, Gail, and two kids—two boys away in Brisbane at boarding school. We send the kids away around ten, so they can get a good education. I was educated at my father's and my grandfather's old school in Melbourne. My son—hopefully sons—will go there too."

"You don't want daughters?" she asked, with a certain charge in her voice.

"Absolutely," he said, and drew a finger down the line of her cheek. "Who wouldn't want a daughter that looked, sounded and acted like you?"

She put up a hand, held it for a moment over his, and then drew his hand down. It was enough to make her breathless. They were still standing in the dressing room—only now she was backed against one of the wardrobes.

"We can't do this," she said, in a strange little whispery voice.

"What *are* we doing?" he whispered back, bending his dark head so it was poised over hers.

"I'm thinking of you as well as myself."

"Why are you so sure I want to make love to you?" He whispered the words in her ear.

She flushed at the mockery. "You're a terrible man!" She plunged forward in flight—only, as he had done once before, he caught her back. This time she put up some resistance, though her excitement was very real. She knew what she wanted even if she acted very differently.

"Stop fighting this." A groan came from deep in his throat, as though all resistance was in vain. "I want you so badly I'm nearly mad with it."

His words expressed exactly what *she* was feeling. It passed understanding, this powerful need. "Is this why you brought me here?"

"Is this why you came?"

She lifted her head to stare into his brilliant eyes. "What do you want out of life, Blaine? *Tell me.*"

His expression was very serious. "A woman to love. A woman I've only imagined up to date. A woman who will have my children and raise them with me—a woman who won't ever leave me. But a woman like you—a woman who lives such a very glamorous lifestyle—could slip out of the grasp of a man like me." He broke off, his voice roughening in concern. "Sienna, what are you crying for?"

She dashed a stray tear from her cheek. "God, I don't know." Tears were a natural response to high emotion.

"Are you crying out of grief for Mark?" He stared down at her.

"More out of pity for myself," she said with a poignant little shrug. "I didn't ask for this, Blaine—for what's happening between us."

"Any more than I did," he answered. "But it's

not as though you can't make your escape. You get on a plane and go home. You take Amanda with you. I'm sorry to say this, but I think Amanda is trouble."

She couldn't move for the tremors in her legs. "*You're* the big trouble," she said.

"You call falling in love *trouble*, do you?"

She searched his taut face. "You're actually admitting you're in love with me?"

"Oh, stop it. Stop it. *Stop it*," he groaned. Desire was building like a fury inside him. Their bodies were almost touching, drawing closer as though magnetized. "Kiss me," he said, low-voiced. "Last time I kissed you. *This* time you kiss me."

"That sounds like an order." As if it mattered.

"It is."

"From a man well used to giving orders."

"And being obeyed," he told her very quietly.

Desire was so immense she could barely contain it. "You know where this will lead?"

"What did you come here for, Sienna?" he countered.

"I couldn't *not* come," she confessed. "That's scary, don't you think?" She couldn't endure not touching him. She put up her hands, her heart beating wildly, pulling his head down to her. "I've never felt like this before." *Never, never, never.*

"I hope you mean that." He wrapped his strong arms around her, drawing her in closer, closer, so she could feel his powerful arousal.

"Sexual attraction is such a lure—even when you can't bring yourself to trust me."

"I can't deny what I feel. *Kiss* me, Sienna," he repeated, this time harshly.

She wanted to so badly she felt naked and exposed. She stood on tiptoe…

Her lips touched very gently on his—so sweet, so silken. Her questing tongue slipped into his mouth, sending off shock waves inside him. Their tongues met in a love dance. He ran his hands down her back, spreading them out to lock over her hips. A moment more and his hands slipped down over the curves of her taut buttocks, lifting her body up to him. His hunger had grown to such an intensity he had to have more of her. Passionate concentration was stamped on his face. With a muttered exclamation he swooped her up like a featherweight and carried her through to his bed.

She lay with one arm flung out, her long rose-gold hair in disarray. He lowered himself onto the bed beside her. There he turned her gently on her side, reaching for the long zipper of her dress. He pulled it down—she helped him—peeling the light, sleeveless dress from her and tossing it away. Then he turned her back to him slowly, his eyes moving over her. Her body was just as beautiful as he'd imagined: the small high breasts, the taut midriff, narrow waist, sleek thighs, and the long, slender length of her legs. She was wearing only bra and matching briefs, as pretty as any bikini. This was a body he didn't yet know. But he *would* know. Oh, *yes*! He wanted desperately to satisfy her. He wanted them both to connect with the moon and the stars. She was a thousand times *more* than his imagination. She was the woman he had been searching for. How could he possibly let her go?

"Make love to me," she whispered, holding up her arms to him. Excitement and sexual hunger radiated from her, unravelling his last scrap of control.

His heart was pounding in his ears. Her voice conveyed the deepest longing, flooding his veins with a kind of exultance. He *would* make love to her. Endlessly. All through the night. Nothing now could stop him.

CHAPTER SEVEN

SOME time in the early hours of the following morning Amanda awoke, feeling an overpowering sense of fright, of things going badly wrong. A glance at the little carriage clock in her room told her it was two-fifty a.m. Wasn't three o'clock some sort of witching hour?

Things she had done came back to haunt her. Things she should have been ashamed of, but hadn't been at the time. The dark side of her ran deep. What was she going to do with her life from now on? She would have to pay for what had happened. Mark was dead. But he had long left her behind. She had been in love with him in the beginning. She would have loved him to the end. Only the woman he'd really wanted was Sienna. She knew—of *course* she knew—Sienna had never given Mark the slightest encouragement. Sienna had gone out of her way to avoid ever being alone with him. But for some twisted reason it gave her great satisfaction to heap blame on her beautiful, gifted, ever-popular cousin. Ever since high school boys had swarmed around Sienna like bees. Was it the honey hair, the honey eyes, the honey voice? She couldn't remember a time when she hadn't felt violently jealous of Sienna.

I love her.

I hate her.

That was the really odd part. She had always relied heavily on Sienna, who had never failed to support her through all her troubles—and there had been many. She felt like talking to Sienna now. Sienna always managed to calm her.

She tossed back the covers like a child desperate for comfort. Sienna would help. She always did.

Only Sienna wasn't in her room. The bed was still made up, the luxurious quilt in place. So where was her sainted cousin?

She's naked in bed with Blaine.

The voice in her head was so loud she had to hold her hands over her ears.

"Bitch!" she shouted into the empty room. "You're going to pay for this."

It was the next day. "Please have a seat, Amanda," Blaine spoke gently, as he showed his half-brother's young widow into his father's old study. She was looking extremely pale. Heartbreaking, really, when he had thought her tough—or at the very least conniving—to the core. Now he felt considerable remorse, looking down at her with a definite softening to his manner. She was such a little bit of a thing, without spark. He supposed she would be very pretty in her way when she was well, but she didn't look well at all, although she should have been pretty much over her jet lag.

What exactly had attracted Mark to her? he wondered, not for the first time.

Amanda was *waiting* to tell him. Her blue eyes lifted to Blaine's face as she began to squeeze tears out of her eyes. It was one of her best tricks. She could sob at will and she was fully prepared to do so. Men melted at a woman's tears. Even Mark had done that when she had accused him of sleeping with Sienna.

"I *wish*!" he had groaned, before getting ready to head out without her.

Some part of her had even been pleased when he had slammed into that tree. He had wronged her, so why shouldn't he be punished? The cruelty of the man! She had never forgiven him for that. She had never even felt a pang when they buried him. Was that *normal*? Mark had been a loser, but his big brother was something else again. Mark's big brother was going to pay up big-time. Why wouldn't he, when he heard her story?

Blaine sat behind his father's massive partner's desk, his eyes trained on Amanda as she literally heaved out a story of treachery.

"Sienna always took what I wanted," she said, the tears pouring down her blanched cheeks. "I know she didn't exactly *mean* to, but it always happened. The day Mark told me he'd only married me to get to Sienna I felt like giving up and killing myself.

"Killing yourself?" Blaine repeated. "How?"

"What?" Why would he speak like that to her?

"How were you going to kill yourself?" he asked.

She hated the fact he looked so *stern*. He wasn't responding as she had hoped.

"I don't know—sleeping pills, a bottle of vodka." She cast about wildly. "You can't image the depth of pain I was in."

"So what you're claiming is that Sienna, who appears devoted to you, was sleeping with your husband?" Blaine asked in a clinically concise voice.

"I know the way it sounds." She shook her head from side to side. "It sounds *terrible*. But I saw them. It was a dreadful affront to my marriage. Sienna didn't love Mark. She was toying with him. She's so beautiful she can have anyone she wants."

"So why would she want Mark?" Blaine asked of Mark's widow, very gravely. "We've just buried him, remember? Do you really want to destroy his image in his family's eyes? Do you want to destroy Sienna?" What *was* going on with this young woman?

Deep in her role, Amanda was incapable of dropping her act. "I *love* Sienna," she said with actual sincerity. "I'll always love her. But she caused me terrible grief. I know she didn't intend for me to catch them out."

Blaine sat back like a judge. "I'm sorry, Amanda, but I can't believe a word of this."

Amanda jerked back in shock. "It's true! It's true!" She was fighting her hardest to convince him. "Why would I lie to you? It wouldn't be right. I have a little more integrity than that. I've asked myself the same question over and over. Why would Sienna do that to me?"

"You mean that which didn't happen?"

She looked at him, so big and powerful. "She's got to you, hasn't she?" She found her most pitiable voice. "She does that—can't you see?"

"No, I can't, Amanda," Blaine said flatly. "I think, very sadly, you've been jealous of your cousin all your life. I know about jealousy and resentment. I know because it happened to me. I had to endure Mark's bitter jealousies and resentments. I bet he filled your ears with all the rotten things I did to him. Jealousy ravaged him like it's ravaging you."

Amanda looked back at him in stunned disbelief. "Are you mad at me, Blaine?"

His eyes on her, he said, "Mad at you? No,

Amanda. I think you need help. I do believe Mark treated you badly. I do believe he fell out of love with you. Mark was never a stayer. Sienna's beauty and her warm personality would have attracted him despite himself. He was drawn to her like a moth to a flame. But then, I imagine any number of young men have been in love with her."

"You too," Amanda accused forlornly. "You're a strong, clever man, but you're not seeing straight on this. I don't blame you. I've seen it all before. I swear everything I've said to you is *true*. I can't offer proof. I can only offer you my word. My word on my child's life." Amanda threw up her blonde head as she proclaimed her pregnant state proudly.

For a moment Blaine was too stunned to speak. "You're pregnant?" he asked finally. Some women bloomed, others could look very wan. Did that explain it?

She nodded, using a handkerchief to bravely wipe away her tears. "Confirmed."

"My God! And Mark is the father?"

Amanda showed more hurt than outrage. "Of

course Mark is the father. What do you take me for? We were still having sex."

"At the same time Mark was having an affair with Sienna?" Blaine asked incredulously. "Come on, now, Amanda."

"Mark and I had sex during that time," Amanda maintained. "Why can't you simply believe me?"

Because it's all bunkum. Instead he asked, "Did Mark know about this baby?"

She shook her head with the saddest expression. "This baby is *our* baby. Hilary's grandchild. Your half-nephew, or whatever the relationship is. There never seemed to be the right time to tell Mark. I hate myself now for not telling him. It might have saved him."

Blaine kept his eyes trained on her. "Are you implying he was suicidal?"

"He couldn't have Sienna, you see."

"Ah, yes," he said, in a voice Amanda didn't much like. "Sienna doesn't know you're pregnant?"

He continued to watch her with those extraordinary diamond-hard eyes. She felt as if they were drilling holes right through her. "I was getting around to telling her," Amanda blurted. "But I've felt such injustice. My own cousin betrayed me. I'll get over it in time. I know I will. But right now—" She broke off. "That's why the money is so important to me, Blaine. I'll have the security and the peace of mind to raise Mark's child. I need someone to love. I desperately need someone to love *me*. My baby will do that."

"You want this baby?"

"Desperately," Amanda said. "I'll have something of my own."

Blaine glanced away, then back at this waif-like little person who clearly needed help. "I had proposed to give you five million, Amanda. That's Australian dollars. You will remarry in time. Invested wisely, five million will keep you nicely."

Amanda sat forward. "Five million for *me*, Blaine? Shouldn't it be a lot more for the baby?"

So she was raising the bar. "Forgive me, but I don't even know if you *are* pregnant, Amanda. I don't even know if the baby's Mark's."

If possible she lost even more colour. "You know it is," she said, sounding unbearably upset. "Sienna will know it's true. Mark may have cast me aside, but I bear his child. I'd like you, Blaine, to take that into consideration."

"And I'd like *you*, Amanda, to keep your very unexpected news to yourself until I have time to sort things out. Can you promise to do that?"

"Of course I'll do that," Amanda said, with tears in her eyes.

Sienna took shot after shot of the wild flowers, standing in the centre of a great circle of pure white everlastings armed with her camera. She bent to break off several paper daisies, which didn't wilt when picked, thrusting them into her hair and her braid. Lines from a poem of William Blake, one of her favourite poets, sprang inevitably to mind.

To see a World in a Grain of Sand,
And Heaven in a Wild Flower,
Hold Infinity in the palm of your hand,
And Eternity in an hour.

She felt extraordinary, standing in the middle of this Outback ocean of wild flowers on the other side of her own world. The truth was she was in a state of euphoria. What had happened between her and Blaine last night had been a colossal, life changing event. Their lovemaking had gone on and on, utterly ravishing to the senses. They hadn't been able to get enough of each other. Passion was a potent force that swept mere mortals away. He knew *exactly* how to kiss her, touch her, caress her. He knew when to allow her to take the lead, and when he had her on her back mastered her so gloriously. Life was so short. Too short for Mark. She fancied she saw his silvery shadow blend in with the mirage. It had never been discussed, but now she had the totally dismaying notion Mark had only married Amanda because she was pregnant. Or had *claimed* to be pregnant.

Now, where had that come from? No one had doubted Amanda. She had suffered her early miscarriage when she was in her bathroom, alone. Sienna had been with her father in New York. Amanda had had to take herself off to a doctor. Not the family doctor, nor even the clinic where he practised.

Sienna clamped the side of her bottom lip between her teeth, trying to thrust her disturbing thoughts away. Of *course* Amanda had been pregnant. She had a vision of herself comforting Amanda when she'd arrived home.

"You'll be fine, Mandy. Fine. Things obviously weren't going well. You'll be pregnant again in no time at all. A good pregnancy. You have to look after yourself."

You ought to speak to Amanda about this, said her inner voice. *But be careful.*

She had spent a lot of time communing with herself this morning. She knew beyond any doubt that she was deeply in love with Blaine. Neither of them had used the words *I love you,* as though each had been waiting for the other to say it first. A continuing relationship would demand serious decisions. She knew Blaine would never—could never—abandon his inheritance. *She* would be the one who had to make the big life-changes. Could she do it?

What a ridiculous question! The answer, overwhelmingly, was *yes.* No place on earth was too far away in the modern world. She would never lose her family and her homeland. Blaine would gain a family and a second home. She could continue her work. She could see exactly how it could be done.

How do you know he wants to marry you?

How can he not marry me if he won't ever let me go?

He'd had no hesitation in assuring her of that. Over and over...all the while raining down kisses on her face, her throat, her breast, moving down over her body.

Blaine had put a station Jeep at her disposal. She was happy with her photo session for the day, so she drove the vehicle to the pink water lily lagoon. She wanted the coolness there after the heat of that brilliant sun pouring down from an opal-blue sky. She parked the Jeep at the top of the slope, and then walked down their trodden path to the sand. Tiny little lilies crushed underfoot gave off a scent so alluring it ought to be bottled. The scent was everywhere. She had left her hat in the vehicle so the light breeze could blow on her bare head.

There was a wonderful sheen like silk on the water. Off to her right the feathery lime-green branches of trees with pale yellow puffs and plumes were dipping and rising with the breeze; water foamed whitely around the standing red boulders that were set at intervals along the stream; more foam lay like lace upon the sand. Such a far, far away place—so beautiful! Already it caught at her heart.

Still lost in her euphoric thoughts, she picked up a pebble, then set it to skip across the surface of the water.

Dream on, Sienna.

It was a marvellous thing to be in love. It had totally changed her and yet she had never felt more *herself*, more womanly, with an endless capacity to satisfy her man. Love stirred the imagination and set the flesh on fire. Her every need had been met by this one man, even into the dawn...

The moment the pebble hit the water a flock of brilliantly plumaged parrots rose up, scattering and screeching as if a bomb had gone off.

"Sorry!" she called apologetically, marking with some wonder the stunning combination of enamelled colours in the sun. Audubon country, she thought. The great French-American John James Audubon, the father of bird-painters, would have found endless inspiration in Australia's Outback. He'd had such a love and fascination with the beauty and dynamics of all species of birds. She did too.

I could paint this place.

Not in the moving depictions created by the country's indigenous people, but in a white woman's way. The ancient landscape was enormously powerful. And she had only seen what amounted to a postage stamp area. She considered herself a woman blessed to have her own passion for the land—a land that couldn't have been more different from what she'd been born to. But it was a truly amazing world, with each country having something wonderful to praise.

Blaine spotted the Jeep at the very spot where he'd thought Sienna might be. Magda had told him Miss Sienna had gone off to "take lots of photographs".

"She is a photographer as well as an artist," Magda had added, with a touch of awe.

He needed to talk to Sienna, and it had to be right away. He had no great faith in Amanda. No great faith in her keeping her momentous news to herself now that her secret was out. Hilary, he realized, would be thrilled out of her mind to know she had a grandchild on the way. It would lessen her deep grief at losing her only son. The huge problem was that Amanda would be going back home to Canada. Any fascination the Outback might have was totally lost on her. He was certain she wouldn't stay. As soon as he gave her the money she would be on her way. *More* money, as well. He was done with being surprised by Mark's widow. Shallowness and greed weren't a good combination. She would want to raise her child back home.

You couldn't totally know a person *ever,* he thought. No way could he read Sienna like a book. But he *had* grasped the fact that Amanda had the same problems with Sienna as Mark had had with him. Amanda might well be a pathological liar. Even so, pathological liars were often believed. That was the truly bizarre part. He could not, *would* not accept his beautiful Sienna had had an affair with Mark, however short-lived. He would *hate* for that to have happened.

Damn it—it didn't happen!

No way would he believe Amanda over Sienna. Mark might well have tried his hardest to develop a relationship—it was the sort of thing Mark had done—but he couldn't for the life of him see

Sienna falling for Mark, let alone betraying her own cousin.

He leaned against the horn to alert Sienna to his presence, then he got out of his vehicle, striding down the coarsely grassed slope. "Sienna!" he called.

She was rushing towards him, electric for him, a radiant smile lighting up her beautiful face, such pleasure in her eyes. "What are you doing here?"

His sober expression brought her up short. "We have to talk," he said quietly, taking her arm.

"What is it? What's wrong?" She had thought he had driven out to the lagoon to meet up with her—marvellous idea. Now it seemed he had something very different on his mind. That was immensely sobering, but sobering things happened all the time. Especially around Amanda.

"It's about Amanda, isn't it?" she guessed, standing very still beside him. "Something was said at your meeting? She's okay, isn't she? She hasn't been terribly well of late."

"I guess that can happen when a woman's pregnant," he answered, his expression more grim than delighted.

For a moment Sienna thought she wasn't hearing right. "Hang on. Amanda told *you* she's pregnant?"

"Such a big event is worth more money. She's pregnant with Mark's child," he said bluntly, wrenched by the thought that Amanda might very well come between them. It could happen. Right or wrong, Sienna was devoted to her cousin.

"Dear God!" Sienna breathed. "I had no idea. Why didn't she say something? She's not taking proper care of herself. That long flight in these early months. Her drinking. Why didn't she say? She should be looking after herself for the baby."

"So there *is* a baby?" he asked.

That struck at her like a blow. "Oh, God, Blaine, you sound so cynical. What's going on here? Didn't she tell you she was? Amanda can be a very secretive little person. She's had one miscarriage, you know."

"No, I *don't* know," he said tersely, relying on his gut feeling that Amanda was a very devious, manipulating young woman. "When was this?"

"Oh, early days!" Sienna threw up a vague hand. "It occurred to me not long after we arrived she might be pregnant—highly irritable, sickly and lying down all the time. But I dismissed it.

Then she goes and tells *you*. I don't get it. I never get it with Amanda."

"I'm not surprised!' he said in his most clipped voice. "I think your cousin is a young woman with lots of problems. I find it near unbearable to mention this, but she's holding to her story that Mark was in love with you. That he only married her to get to you."

For a moment Sienna felt like screaming. Turning on a tantrum like Amanda, who was right in her element screaming. Only Sienna wasn't made like that. But she *was* driven to throwing her arms impotently into the air. "He married her because she told him she was pregnant," she said. "Honestly, Amanda might be my cousin, but she's the most appalling troublemaker.'

"There's always a scrap of truth in a mountain of lies," he offered starkly, trying to cope with his own massive upset. The thought in his mind was that Amanda was a liar who was going to cause more problems for his family.

"At least tell me what she said," Sienna begged.

All the radiant pleasure was drained out of her face. That hurt him. "Perhaps we need to talk about it for it to go away," he said, and drew in a long, determined breath. "Last night meant everything to me, Sienna."

There was no doubting his sincerity. "It meant everything to *me*, Blaine. Yet you can still harbour some element of doubt about me?"

"No, no!" He shook his handsome head vigorously. "I *don't* doubt you. But I still don't know exactly what happened between you and Mark. It's preying on my mind, Sienna. Can't you see that?"

"Are you sure you *want* to know?" Her voice was a challenging mix of distress and deep disappointment.

"Whatever happened, I won't let you go." He turned her towards him, holding onto her shoulders. She had picked some white paper daisies, popped them into her thick braid and the open top buttonhole of her shirt. They still clung to her. Why not? He thought her the most beautiful creature he had ever seen. How could he ever cage such a woman? "Amanda claims she surprised you and Mark," he managed, after a moment.

Sienna closed her eyes. "She *did*," she admitted. She opened her eyes again and fixed them on his brooding face. "I'd gone over to their apartment to deliver a birthday present for Amanda from my mother. I expected her to be there, only Mark was the one at home. Amanda had been delayed, he said, doing some extra shopping. I wanted to leave the present, saying I had to be on my way, only Mark saw it as a priceless opportunity for us to be together. He thought himself attractive to women. He *was* attractive to women. I had seen that for myself. But he was never attractive to me. I spotted something not quite right in Mark from the word go. Amanda isn't a strong person. She needed balance. We knew she wouldn't get it from Mark, nor he from her. But she didn't listen. She's *never* listened, come to think of it. She was—"

Blaine cut her off, steel in his tone. "I don't want to hear about Amanda, only *you*."

"Me?" She gave him a long stare, but she was the first to look away. "Okay, Blaine, you asked for it. Mark was in the mood for games, but my mind was concentrated on getting away. He told me if I could only relax he would make me feel good."

Blaine had to fight hard to control his rush

of anger. "But you couldn't have kept silent, Sienna?"

"Of course I didn't. But Mark was determined. I was wasting my breath."

"What sort of a fool was he?" Blaine groaned in despair. "A woman like you, with your family, a father and brother to answer to. Obviously he didn't give a damn about betraying his wife."

Sienna too was struggling to compose herself. "Blaine," she said, more calmly, "you were his half-brother. You knew what he was like. Mark didn't really care about anyone. He didn't obey the rules like the rest of us. He didn't even know them. He genuinely thought he could do what he liked. I think he planned the whole thing. I'd rung *Amanda* earlier in the day to say I would drop the present over. Mark made sure he was there and Amanda wasn't."

"So what happened? "Blaine asked with great insistency.

There was a golden flame in her eyes. "He over-powered me. That's what happened. He slammed me into a wall. He held both my hands behind my back. He manhandled me and took great pleasure in it. He was much stronger—" She broke off, swallowing on a parched throat. She was growing steadily more agitated. What if Blaine didn't believe her? She didn't think she could cope with that. Amanda could be terribly, harmfully convincing. "Look, I don't want to talk about this."

"I don't either," he responded tautly. "But we have to. Let me share your pain."

"*Shame*, you mean!" she cried out from the depths of her wounded soul. When would this finally end?

Blaine felt as if he had swallowed acid. It was burning into his gut. "You're telling me Mark raped you?" he asked, a terrible tension in his face and lean body. "My God, if he were still around I'd strangle him with my bare hands."

"Don't say that! You wouldn't do it. Though I'm sure you'd give him the hiding of a lifetime. It didn't get that far, Blaine. You must believe that—for me, for yourself, even for Mark. Amanda arrived on the scene. Only there wasn't time for Mark to break away. Amanda caught him with his hand down the front of my dress. He had a bruising grip on my breast. When she saw that, Amanda started screaming and raving. Then she started throwing things. She wouldn't stop. She was out of control. She seemed desperate to hurt me. *Me*, not Mark. Can you beat that? He was the predator. I was the victim. But it was *me* she wanted to hurt. Oddly enough, it was Mark who stood between us, turning of all things into my protector. At least he had some remnant of decency left. He *told* Amanda it was all his fault, though she wasn't happy with that. No way! I have to be punished for the rest of my life. Mark told her he lost his head."

"Do you think that exonerated him?" Blaine asked in a white fury.

"No, of course not! But women are always under threat from a man's physical power, Blaine. Look how tall and big and strong you are compared with me. You could overpower me with one arm behind your back. There's a violence in men and boys that's hidden behind their attractive white grins. A dear friend of mine was raped in college by one of our top athletes. She told no one at the time. She only told me years later. She was still traumatized. He's a successful lawyer now, no doubt still taking the women he wants. The thing is, women are always at a man's mercy for that very good reason—their greatly superior physical strength."

He looked down on her bright head, the daisies a pure white contrast to the glowing amber of her hair. He remembered his first sight of her. He had known her then. His physical self and his mind, his spirit. "For God's sake, Sienna, the world is full of good, decent men," he protested. "Caring men, protective men, family men, husbands, fathers, partners. Most men aren't potential rapists. Surely you've learned that? I could never harm you. Do you think I could? I could never harm any woman. Take that as an absolute. How could Mark have assaulted you, even if he hadn't intended something more terrible?"

She gave a brittle laugh. "Well, we don't know that, do we? But Amanda has never let me forget that day she walked in on us. She *knows*—Mark told her—I was the innocent party. She *knows* me. Yet every now and again some demon in her rises up."

"So just think how *women* can and do behave! Women have a different kind of power. They know how to use it like the crack of a whip. Your cousin needs help." Blaine's voice carried outrage, not pity. "Ah, come here to me," he said, his taut expression softening. "I'm sorry. So sorry." He drew her tightly into his arms, resting his chin on the top of her head. "What are we going to do about this?"

She lifted her head to him, all her nerves fluttering. Right at that moment she was only interested in the two of them. Amanda and her pregnancy could wait. God knew how far along she was. It had taken a great deal to force that sickening incident with Mark out of her, but now she was glad she'd told Blaine. It was as though a heavy burden had been lifted from her. Amanda would have to give up her baseless accusations or forfeit their relationship. She knew Amanda would have done her worst to damage her and her good name. It was as though Amanda saw it as her entitlement to bring her down.

A look of remembered rapture was transforming her expression, bringing back her natural radiance. "More to the point, what are we going to do about *us*?"

He took her beautiful face between his hands, amazed the woman of his dreams had come into his life. Had the gods brought her to him? Would she stay? His whole body burned with desire and love. "I want an *us* more than I want anything, Sienna. It's hard to imagine how I could go on without you. But I know there are so many things we need to work out."

"As long as you believe in me?" She stared up into his glittering eyes.

"I believe you're someone rare and precious," he said. "I'm fiercely protective of you. I only hope I can work to dissolve your pain. I have to admit to feeling a degree of guilt because Mark was my half-brother. What he did was an affront to you, his wife, and to our families. It was vicious and cowardly, to my mind. I'm going to do everything I can to make it up to you."

"So kiss me," she implored, drawing his eyes to her softly alluring waiting mouth. "And don't stop. Please don't stop."

They were together. An opal blue sky was above them. The wild fragrant bush was around them. She was where she wanted to be, sealed off and safe in Blaine's powerful arms. She didn't want to solve the problem of Amanda right now.

Nothing mattered but Blaine and his belief in her. She had thought she would never find the love she craved. She had thought she would never find that one perfect-to-her man.

She was ecstatic to find herself blissfully wrong.

CHAPTER EIGHT

SHE drove back to the homestead, her flesh tingling, a smile on her mouth.

Blaine had things to do that afternoon. He had to organize an overdue cattle drive. With Katajangga Station covering some four million acres it was a huge job to chase and then drive out sections of the herd that had sought a hiding place in the wild scrub. Often the cattle travelled over many miles into the desert fringe. He was planning on taking the helicopter up and letting his stockmen on the ground—some on horseback, others on motorbikes—know the exact location of the various hide-outs. A chopper was indispensable on a working station, for mustering and aerial views of the vast area. Driving large numbers of unwilling cattle back to holding yards closer to home territory was a hard and often dangerous job, but his men loved it, he said. This was the place they wanted to be. Theirs was the best job in the world. They couldn't do this one in a few days. Some of the men would have to camp out—most probably for weeks.

When Sienna returned to the homestead she found to her astonishment that Amanda was sitting companionably with Hilary over a light lunch. Would wonders never cease? Amanda was pretty remarkable in her way, Sienna thought, heartened by the way Amanda had pulled herself together. Amanda could act sweetly, or act badly. There was nothing much in between. Today she had put on a very pretty sundress, no doubt for her interview with Blaine, washed her hair and applied just the right amount of make-up. Make-up made a big difference to her. She looked much more herself.

Hilary looked up with a bright tremulous smile that expressed her pleasure in having Amanda share some quality time with her. "Have you had lunch, dear?" she asked Sienna.

"I'd love a sandwich." Sienna smiled back. "How are you today, Hilary?" she asked with genuine concern. She had thought Hilary might fall apart.

"Coping better," Hilary said, reaching to cover Amanda's small hand that was lying on the table with her own.

"I'm so pleased to hear it," Sienna responded, noting the gesture. "And you, Amanda?" Her eyes moved to her cousin. "You look much better."

"I feel much better," Amanda said, giving Hilary's frail hand a squeeze. So she *did* have a heart! Then she looked back at Sienna, as though waiting for some reaction from her.

One wasn't forthcoming. "I'll go through to the kitchen. Be back in a minute," Sienna promised.

Blaine had told her before they parted company that he had specifically asked Amanda not to mention her pregnancy to Hilary until he'd had time to think things through, and Amanda would have to be seriously deranged to ignore his express wishes. The fact it might *cost* her would act as a deterrent. Amanda had learned early to act appropriately when it was in her own best interests. Obviously she had grasped the fact she had to get the Kilcullen family on side, and it was heartening to know she had already made an attempt. That was a big step forward.

Marcia was due home some time that afternoon—Joanne, who had her pilot's licence, would be flying her in. But whether Joanne intended to stay over she didn't know. Anyway, Amanda had known from the very beginning about Mark's abandoned fiancée. It hadn't worried her then. It wouldn't worry her now. Amanda operated on a different system from most people.

An hour or so later Sienna drove down to the airstrip to pick up Marcia and Joanne. Truth be told, although she'd wanted to do the pick-up, she had found Amanda's newly realized empathy for her mother-in-law a bit on the cloying side. Amanda was acting out of character, but Hilary was clearly taken in. Sienna, however, had her cousin's measure. The show of togetherness was contrived. Of course she couldn't fail to grasp the significance. Amanda was carrying Hilary's grandchild. That put her in a powerful position, and maybe Amanda craved power.

Amanda—a mother! Maybe it would be the making of her. She would have to take responsibility for her life and that of her unborn child. Sienna couldn't ignore the thought that Kilcullen money would help, though her own family would never see Amanda go short or without support. Had Mark known about his child? Surely he had not. How far along *was* Amanda anyway? She was still very slight. No baby bump. At the first opportunity she and Amanda had to talk.

Sienna pushed her sense of hurt away. She had never thought for a moment that Amanda would keep the news of her pregnancy from her. The fact of the matter was Amanda *had*.

Why, exactly? Why had Amanda felt it necessary to keep her pregnancy under wraps? Because she had miscarried in the past and wanted to be very sure before she announced the big event? Or because Mark's tragic early death had delivered a numbing blow? Sienna concluded it was a combination of both.

A white, blue and yellow-striped Cessna was standing like a big bird on the concrete apron. Marcia and Joanne were lolling in the shade of a giant hangar.

Sienna slammed the door of the Jeep and hurried towards them. "Hi!"

They moved towards her as one, no formality between any of them. "Thanks for coming for us," Marcia said, giving Sienna a spontaneous kiss on the cheek.

"No trouble at all. How are you?"

"Getting there," Marcia said.

"I have to return home," Joanne told Sienna, bestowing upon her another friendly kiss. "Always things to do around the station. But I'd love a cuppa."

"Me too." Marcia lightly touched Sienna's shoulder. Despite the odds all three young women were at ease with each other. "How's Mum?"

"She's coping better today," Sienna said, stowing Marcia's overnight bag. "She looks better."

"Amanda up and about yet?" Marcia asked, getting into the front passenger seat, while Joanne clambered in the back.

"Actually, she and Hilary have been enjoying lunch and a long conversation," Sienna said, switching on the ignition. "I've been out taking photographs of the wild flowers, the great gardens of the desert and the amazing landscape."

"I'd love to see them when they're ready," Joanne piped up. "Amanda knows about me? About me and Mark?" she asked.

"Yes, Joanne," Sienna said. "You have no concerns there."

"You *hope*!" said Marcia, in a decidedly unconvinced voice. "I have my own opinion of Amanda, and I bet I'm right. She's probably come round because she thinks Blaine is going to set her up for life."

"Come on, Marcy, why take it out on Sienna?" Joanne hastily intervened, leaning forward to make a protest.

"Sorry, Sienna," Marcia apologized. "I don't want to offend *you*. I like you. But you know better than I do that your cousin is one big crate of trouble."

"Oh, Marcy!" Another wail of protest from Joanne.

"A harsh judgement, Marcia," Sienna said.

"I know. But it could be the truth,'" Marcia said, in a worried voice. "I know in my bones Amanda doesn't mean well." She actually gave a shudder.

Sienna glanced across at Mark's twin. Marcia wasn't Mark's mirror image, but the resemblance was very strong. Some facets of the manner as well. "Take it easy now, Marcia," she said gently. "I'm here."

"To act as a buffer?" Marcia shot her a wry glance. "I don't know why you do it."

"You know why. Amanda is family. My parents took her in when she was a little girl. I can't just up and abandon her."

"I hope you don't have to." Marcia spoke very seriously. "But watch your back. You're too kind, Sienna. Maybe for your own good."

"Marcy, Sienna knows what she's about." Once more Joanne, well used to her friend and her often alarmingly straight talk, intervened.

"It's okay, Joanne," Sienna said soothingly. "I understand how Marcia feels. Mark and Amanda didn't handle family matters well. But there are a few things you have to know."

"Like what?" Marcy sat bolt upright in alarm.

"Blaine will explain." Sienna kept her voice re-laxed. "Now for the most important thing," she said, as they swept through the open gates of the compound. "A cup of tea."

"Lovely!" Joanne breathed. "When do you think you can come over, Sienna?" she asked. "You can't possibly go home without a visit."

"Sienna is going to stay a good while—aren't you, Sienna?" Marcia stated, as though it were a *fait accompli.* "Amanda might want to fly off just as soon as she can, but you don't have to. Believe me, we've got lots to show you—haven't we, Jo?"

"Plenty!" Joanne smiled. "Like, for example, the Red Centre, Uluru and Katajuta."

"That's Ayer's Rock and the Olgas," Marcia supplied. "Kata means many. We have many rock formations on Katajangga. If you want to see some truly wonderful desert rock formations you have to visit our Ancient Domes. Blaine will arrange it all. I know he wants you to see as much as you possibly can before you go home. I wish you weren't going home, actually. You and Blaine seem to click. I wish I could find someone *I* could click with," she supplied confidentially.

"Me too," sighed Joanne from the back seat.

"It will happen." Sienna used her most reassuring tone. "But first you might have to widen your horizons. At least in terms of meeting people. You'd both be very welcome to visit my country. It's very beautiful, very big, and very diverse. I have a large apartment in Vancouver—three bedrooms: master, guest, and the other I use as my study. But there's also a comfortable sofabed. You could use the apartment as a *pied à terre.*"

"That sounds very French." Joanne laughed, fascinated like most people by an authentic French accent.

"I'm bilingual," Sienna replied. "Think about it."

"Gosh, you won't have to ask *me* twice," Marcia's whole face had lit up. It was such a transformation.

"Me either!" Joanne chortled. "Canada, here we come!"

Amanda had settled right into her good behaviour, even exhibiting a few little airs and graces that went over very well with Hilary. Sienna couldn't help noticing Amanda was getting far more attention from Hilary than her own daughter. Sienna's kindly impression of Hilary slipped a bit as a consequence. But she did find herself breathing a great sigh of relief. Maybe Amanda's morning sickness—whatever—had settled as well, and she was on the road to recovery. There was a whole list of questions she wanted to ask her cousin at the first opportunity, but she had the nagging idea Amanda was putting any and all questioning off.

Amanda did, however, apologize very sweetly

to Marcia for what Marcia might have thought of as her "stand-offishness". Her nerves had been shot to pieces, she explained. Joanne received an apology as well. Both young women accepted the apologies more gracefully than Amanda might have expected or deserved—although Sienna intercepted a very enigmatic smile from Marcia. She appeared to have summed Amanda up from their first brief meeting, the day after their arrival. Sienna was vividly reminded of how very quickly she had summed up Mark.

Joanne flew home no more than an hour later. Blaine hadn't arrived back at the homestead.

"He'll come in at dusk," Marcia told Sienna. "Dinner at seven. Come down a bit earlier," she invited, before turning to Amanda. "You are having dinner with us, Amanda?"

"Of course I am." Amanda appeared entirely at ease. "I'm feeling very much better."

Under her pretty pink blusher Sienna thought her cousin was still looking pale. But that was only to be expected. She was starting to feel real concern about Amanda's drinking. She felt obliged to speak up as soon as she got the chance.

Walking along the upper floor gallery to their

beautiful guestrooms, Sienna took Amanda's hand—much as she had done when they were children and she was the elder, the one in the lead. But Amanda shook it off.

"I don't want to talk now, Sienna," she said.

Sienna laughed in disbelief. "But this is incredible news, Mandy. You're pregnant! Only it's such good news I'm hurt you didn't confide in me. Or Mum—or anyone."

"What's good about it?" Amanda turned on her, all her sweetness and light hardening into an all too familiar resentment.

"I don't understand you," Sienna said. "You loved Mark once. This is his child. You may have been feeling sickly but your tummy will settle. And just think when the baby comes. A beautiful baby to love and cherish!"

"Oh, shut up," Amanda said, in a rude, angry-sounding voice.

Sienna pulled a disgusted face. She saw that her cousin's calm was shattering. "So, do I take that as proof positive you don't want your child?" she asked, very quietly.

"I told you, Sienna." Amanda gritted her small white teeth. "I don't want to talk about it. I want to get out of here as quickly and as painlessly as I can."

"In which case I should tell you I'm not coming with you," Sienna announced. "I'm staying on for a while."

"Blaine, of course!" Amanda sneered. "You're as bold as brass. You're sleeping with him already. Now, that's what I call fast work."

"Call it what you like, Amanda—and *you* would know." Immediately the words were out of her mouth Sienna regretted them as a cheap shot.

Amanda's brittle tone abruptly broke, and she gave a kind of strangled whimper. "You couldn't let me travel all the way home alone, Sienna. I'm *pregnant*." She ran her hands wildly through her pretty blonde curls. "The very time I need you, you propose to *abandon* me?"

Sienna stared at her cousin in consternation. Amanda was visibly trembling. "Look, don't upset yourself, Mandy," she relented. "I can see you need someone at this time. But we have to strike a bit of a balance here. It won't hurt you to stay on. How far along are you? Hilary has brightened no end, just being able to talk to you.

Just think how excited she'll be when she hears the good news."

"Damn Hilary," Amanda exclaimed, her voice full of venom. They were now at her door. "I'm going to lie down for a half-hour," she said. "So don't come in."

"Okay." Sienna was determined not to get into an argument. "But there are a few things we need to clear up, Mandy, before you make your announcement. You still haven't told me—how far along are you?"

"You suspect I'm *not* pregnant?" Amanda's petite body had turned stiff as a board.

"Amanda, I didn't say that." Sienna shook her head, perplexed. "I merely asked how many months. You miscarried once. You have to be doubly careful."

Amanda swung about like a defiant child. "You're supposed to be my cousin—my best friend. Why can't you simply support me?"

Sienna put a hand to her cousin's back, feeling the bones like little jutting chicken wings. "Mandy, I *am* supporting you. I've always supported you. Settle down, now."

"Just leave me alone!" Amanda opened her bedroom door. "My baby's conception was no act of love."

Sienna froze. "For God's sake, Amanda," she muttered, low-voiced. "You're not going to put the blame on your innocent unborn babe? When *was* this anyway?" She frowned, her instincts suddenly kicking in. "Mark was away for a month or more when he took that hospitality job in Banff."

Amanda didn't answer. She darted away into her bedroom and slammed the heavy door. Sienna heard the key turn in the lock. Chills were breaking over her in waves. She rattled the doorknob, feeling a great sense of urgency, but Amanda ignored her.

"Come on, Mandy," Sienna urged. *"Please."*

She heard Amanda's near-hysterical reply. "Go away!"

Sienna went. She feared making matters worse. Amanda was so unpredictable. And being pregnant she would be at the mercy of her raging hormones. Alarmed on a number of counts, Sienna walked down the corridor to her own bedroom.

The voice inside her head spoke out.

You're right to question this pregnancy.

A pregnancy Amanda had kept secret from all

of them. Yet this very day she had confided in Blaine. Could it possibly be a trick to extract more money? She couldn't accept that. Amanda wasn't *that* unbalanced. But she was a very vulnerable little person. Amanda had to take care of herself.

What Sienna didn't realize or take into account was that *she* was the one who needed to take care...

By eight o'clock they were all assembled in the Great Room. One of Magda's young staff members carried around canapés on a silver tray—delicious little morsels. Blaine had been pouring a glass of white wine for Hilary when Sienna reached the bottom of the staircase, walking across the room to join them.

"A glass of wine for you, Sienna?" he asked, waiting for the exact moment when the light from the chandelier fell over her radiant hair. "This is a Chardonnay, but I can get you something else."

"Chardonnay will be fine." Sienna smiled even though she didn't particularly like Chardonnay. She didn't feel sufficiently at ease to ask for anything else.

Seated beside Hilary on the sofa facing the massive piled stone fireplace, Amanda was watching them both very closely, gauging their reactions.

There she is, making another grand entrance. Yet another man in thrall. And what a man! There's nothing fair in life.

Amanda downed her wine in a single gulp. Sienna had told her many times that alcohol made her face take on a definite pallor, but who cared? She needed a drink. Sienna was wearing one of those silk dresses that looked like *nothing* on the hanger until she put it on. This was in a shade of garnet that shouldn't have gone with her hair, but did. Sienna was just *too* perfect. She, Amanda, was the one who'd had the utterly demoralizing task of growing up with such perfection. She remembered how Mark had always bitterly bemoaned walking in his half-brother's tall shadow. It had been just the same with her. Sienna had actually ruined her life in a way.

She had been feeling okay, buoyed up by the thought of the money she was about to get, but now her mood was descending into the doldrums. She could find no pleasure in the thought of the baby. How could she? She had been careless. Upstairs in the bathroom she had stared at her naked body. Hard to believe she was pregnant, but it wasn't a state of mind. In a few weeks she would be starting to show.

"Are you all right?" Blaine asked Sienna quietly as he passed her a crystal wine glass.

She moved closer to him. They were standing by the long sideboard that held the drinks and canapés. "I haven't had a chance to speak to Amanda," she said, as though that grieved her. "Or rather she didn't want to speak to me. I hope she's not going to make any announcement over dinner. Are *you*?" She stared into his dynamic face intently.

For once she saw him falter, his expression darkening. "*I* won't be saying anything, Sienna. Amanda really ought to tell everyone herself. I'm worried that she hasn't confided in you. That's odd. I'm worried she might just blurt her news out."

"Would it be so bad?" Sienna asked, although she also had a fear of her cousin's bent for duplicity.

Involuntarily Blaine brought up his hand, touched her cheek. "You look lovely," he said, low-voiced. He couldn't help himself. She looked so beautiful, so graceful with her lovely hair pinned up. Her silk dress, in a colour that suited her rare colouring, lightly skimmed her slender body, but anyone looking at her would realize just how beautiful her body was. *He* certainly knew. He had never thought his own body would feel incomplete without being inside the body of the woman he loved. He had the mad urge to leave the rest of them to it and take Sienna off. But he couldn't do that. He hoped Amanda had taken him seriously when he told her to keep silent until the appropriate moment...

Magda brought in little baked tournedos of Tasmanian salmon for the entrée, a lamb dish for the main. While they waited for dessert to be served Amanda suddenly picked up a spoon and struck the side of her crystal wine glass. The ping startled Hilary, at one end of the long rectangular table, who looked at her in surprise.

"Yes, dear? You have something to say?"

Blaine braced himself. "What is it, Amanda?" he asked, in a voice that would have stopped a more perceptive person.

"Yes, what is it?" Marcia spoke up too. It sounded like a challenge.

Sienna swallowed hard, knowing Amanda had the bit between her teeth.

"I'm having a baby," Amanda announced, straightening up and holding her head high.

"Oh!" Hilary threw up both her hands in absolute delight. "You're having a baby?" she echoed. "My son's baby?"

"Satisfied, Amanda?" Marcia asked, very tightly. "You're the centre of attention now. Did you know about this, Sienna?" She looked across the table at Sienna, who appeared stricken.

"Only today," Sienna confirmed. "Blaine asked me not to say anything. He felt Amanda should make the announcement."

"Oh, I couldn't be happier!" Hilary cried. She pushed her carver chair back and rushed to Amanda, putting her arms around Amanda's delicate shoulders. "This is wonderful news, Amanda."

"It's certainly news," Blaine said.

"I desperately need some good news." Tears of joy had sprung into Hilary's eyes.

"Don't we all?" Blaine leaned back in his chair, an imposing and very sombre figure.

"You don't look too enthusiastic at the thought of becoming an aunt." Amanda threw Marcia her own challenging glance.

"I expect I'll perk up," Marcia said. "Personally, I don't think you should have kept your news secret, Amanda. How far along are you? There's not a trace of a baby bump yet."

"Well, this *is* my first child," Amanda said.

"But you suffered an earlier miscarriage?" Blaine cut in.

"I wasn't going to bring that up, Blaine." Amanda tutted.

"Well, we're very, *very* glad you have now, my dear," Hilary said, returning to her chair. "I think this calls for champagne?" She looked rather glassy-eyed down the table to Blaine.

"Not terribly appropriate right now, Hilary," Blaine told her quietly.

"Well, haven't you turned out the surprise packet, Amanda?" Marcia said, abruptly rising to her feet. "I wonder if you'll all excuse me? I'm not in the mood for a celebration. We've only just buried my twin."

"You weren't all that close, though, were you?" Amanda said. "Life goes on, Marcia."

Sienna tried to catch Amanda's eye. Failed.

Marcia drew in a harsh breath. "Don't we need some *proof* you're pregnant?" she asked sharply. "Don't we need some proof, if you are pregnant, that the baby is Mark's? I'm not getting good vibes about this. My twin's shadow is not at rest."

Amanda gasped. At the same moment Blaine snapped his fingers—hard. His eyes were glittering like diamonds in the dark tan of his face. "That will do, Marcy," he said. "You're excused."

Sienna sat very still, staring at her clasped hands resting on the linen and lace tablecloth.

"What are you doing, Sienna?" Amanda turned on her cousin, her tone almost a taunt. "Praying she'll cool off?"

Blaine pushed back in his chair. "I think we might hold the dessert, Hilary," he said, throwing his linen napkin down on the table, then standing up. "Sienna, let's take a short walk." He put out an imperative arm.

She went to him.

"I never thought my news would cause such a

rumpus," Amanda said to Hilary, raising her fair brows.

"No, indeed!" Hilary was staring at Blaine in utter astonishment. "Blaine, whatever is the matter?"

"I'll tell you. He thinks I was mad to tell you without his approval." Amanda leaned towards Hilary confidingly. She was convinced she now had Hilary eating out of her hand.

"*Mad* being the operative word." Blaine looped his hand around Sienna's wrist. He knew she was making a real effort to remain quiet.

Marcia wasn't sure about this pregnancy. He couldn't quite believe in it either. Only Sienna could get to the bottom of things. Amanda might well be delusional. Stranger things had happened.

Sienna had never seen so brilliant a sky. It was packed with stars. In an effort to ease the tension between them, she tilted her head upwards. "I don't find it all that easy to locate the Southern Cross," she said. "It seems to be in a different position each night."

"That's because the stars of the Southern Cross, like all stars, rotate throughout the night," Blaine explained. "The location depends on what time of night you're trying to find it. I'll show you." He turned her gently by the shoulders, pointing a finger at the great glittering river of stars that made up the Milky Way. "The Cross is in the middle of the Milky Way. It's the most famous constellation in the Southern Hemisphere. Small compared to other constellations, but it's made up of some of the brightest stars in the heavens. That's Acrus up there. See the very bright one? Some people think it resembles a kite more than a cross. See the two bright stars trailing the kite? They're called pointers. That's how you know for sure you're looking at the Southern Cross."

"I see it clearly now," she said. "I was—"

He stopped her by kissing her, his mouth hard on hers, thrillingly passionate. He held her very closely. She clung to him while he buried his face in her sweet-smelling hair. "What's it going to take to get Amanda to confide in you?" he asked.

She stared up at him in a kind of anguish. "She *is* pregnant, Blaine. It's wrong of us to doubt her."

He gave a harsh laugh. "Marcy certainly doubts her. The twins mightn't have got on, but believe me they were *close*. When they were kids one could finish the other one's sentence. You don't think Amanda could be delusional?"

Sienna shook her head. "No! She's pregnant, all right. But there is the possibility she's not all that happy about it. It's a very bad time for her— losing Mark, especially the way she did."

"I'm like Marcy," Blaine said. "I don't trust Amanda at all."

"I'm sorry. Maybe you think I shouldn't have brought her here?"

"Sienna, *I* was the one who asked her here. She was Mark's wife, even if he didn't feel much love for her."

Disturbing thoughts were pressing in on Sienna. "Life. Death. New life. How did I get so deeply involved in all this?"

"Do you wish we hadn't met?"

"No, never. But—"

"There shouldn't be a *but*, Sienna. Your cousin has a plan, and part of that plan is to stop our relationship going any further."

"So what am I supposed to do? Abandon her?"

He pulled her back into him. Kissed her again. "I want you to come to me tonight. Will you?"

There was nothing she wanted more, yet she felt

compelled to say, "Maybe I should stay close to Amanda." She looked up at him, and he cursed softly beneath his breath.

"For God's sake, Sienna," he cried in exasperation. "You treat your cousin more like a child than a woman."

"I have a responsibility towards her." Sienna felt very much on the defensive. "More so now that she's expecting."

"Which she failed to tell you."

His tone was so terse she could feel her heart hammering violently in her breast. "I don't want us to fight, Blaine."

"I don't want to fight either." He trapped her in his gaze. "I want to make love. I want to make love to you so much I don't think I could get through the night without you. I won't let your cousin destroy what we have."

"Blaine, Amanda is nowhere near as conniving as you think," she said, sickly aware of the hard glint of scepticism in his eyes. "She's vulnerable and in need of my support. Can't you see that?'

He could feel the hot blood rising; forced it down. "Okay. I don't want to upset you. Amanda should be very thankful she has you. You might tell her that if she wants me back on side she had better have a long talk with you. You saw how thrilled Hilary was at her news. Is Amanda going to tell us next she's going home and won't be back?"

"She *will* want to go home," Sienna was obliged to point out.

"Is that what you want too?" He was able to mock himself. All he wanted now was to have Sienna. He didn't want a life without her. Only she had to want that too. Otherwise it would never work.

Dreams were abandoned all the time.

Blaine was reluctant to let her go, and Sienna went upstairs feeling terribly torn. But she had a duty to her cousin and she wasn't going to allow Amanda to put her off. They needed to talk. And first she had to establish how far along her pregnancy was. She wondered if Amanda had consulted a doctor—what doctor?—before undertaking the long flight. She couldn't be even three months. She wasn't showing in any way, even when down to her bra and knickers. Sienna had to understand what was going on.

"Amanda?" She knocked on the bedroom door, listening for a response.

There was none. But she knew Amanda was in there.

Pregnancy could be a big upheaval in a woman's life. So many changes taking place in her body. Maybe Amanda found the prospect of raising her child alone very daunting? The fact she had been suffering morning sickness would have affected her moods. Sienna was roused to sympathy. Amanda would have to stay on until a doctor gave her clearance to make the long journey back home. She had, after all, suffered one miscarriage, and she had never had robust health. Sienna felt the weight of responsibility keenly.

Once inside her own bedroom, she made the decision to walk along the deck to Amanda's bedroom. She should have done that in the first place, since Amanda had decided not to let her in. The big question was *why*?

The French doors were open to the night. She stepped into the bedroom to find Amanda lolling on the bed in her nightgown, her fingertips playing some sort of tattoo on her stomach. "Hi!" she said laconically.

Amanda swung her legs out of bed so abruptly she knocked over a crystal tumbler on the bedside table. "How dare you invade my privacy?"

"Get real!" Sienna put up a staying hand. "This is no time to go on a drinking binge, Amanda," she said, eyeing the fallen tumbler. "What are you thinking of? We have to talk. You seem to have a problem. What is it?"

"Problem? *Exactly.* I'm seriously screwed," Amanda burst out bitterly.

Sienna felt a great stab of alarm. "How's that? Come on—tell me. I'll do everything I can to help you. Are you frightened of this pregnancy? I can understand that."

"Did you *see* Hilary?" Now, unbelievably, Amanda sounded amused. "I could live off her for ever."

Sienna stared back at her cousin in astonishment. "Mandy, what are you talking about?"

Amanda laughed. "Hilary, of course. She's thrilled out of her mind. Not that bitch Marcia. Or your big-time boyfriend. Who does he think he is, anyway?"

"He *knows* who he is, Amanda," Sienna shot back. "The question is, who are *you*? I can't believe you told Blaine without telling me. Did you see a doctor before we left Canada?"

"Are you crazy?" Amanda asked, pulling on her robe.

"I'm not crazy. Are you? How far along are you?"

"Goodness, I don't know. Eight weeks, something like that."

"You're not sure?" Sienna asked incredulously.

"I'm sure I'm pregnant, if that's what you mean," Amanda sneered. "I did a home test. It was valid. What's bugging you, anyway?"

"I'm worried about you," Sienna said. "You should stay here until you're three months at least. That's if you want to go home?"

"Of course I want to go home," Amanda retorted, her tone very cold. "And I *am* going—believe me. As soon as I get the money."

"The money? What the hell are you playing at?" Sienna asked. "This isn't making a lot of sense. When was Mark in Banff?"

Amanda turned ashen. "Don't know. My memory isn't all that reliable these days."

Sienna was determined to get an answer. "I was in Toronto, wasn't I?"

"What the hell does it matter?" Amanda snarled.

"It matters a great deal." Sienna was trying very hard to keep calm. "Mandy, this isn't Mark's baby, is it?" She was playing on no more than a gut feeling.

Only Amanda's small face turned stony. "It is as far as the Kilcullens are concerned."

Sienna put her hands to her head. "God, I don't believe this! You were *lying*? You honestly believe you can put one over on them? How stupid can you be?"

"I'm not stupid at all. I'm going to get the money—which seems reasonable as Hilary is the grandmamma. Hilary is going to see to it."

Sienna stared at Amanda as though she were a total stranger. "You can't allow Hilary to go on believing you're expecting *her* grandchild."

"Why not? It happens all the time," Amanda retorted.

"So who *is* the father?"

"Just a guy." Amanda shrugged.

"Do I know him?"

"No. And he's never going to know anything about it. I don't actually want this baby. I don't fancy playing Mummy. But right now a baby is my trump card."

"You have to be losing your mind," Sienna uttered very bleakly. "Amanda, I have to intervene. I can't allow you to deceive this family."

"I'm confident you will, Sienna," Amanda tossed back at her. "You've always looked out for me."

"Maybe that was a huge mistake! Shut up now," she begged. "I have to think."

Amanda did.

Sienna fell into an armchair, trying hard to clear her swimming head. "I can't allow this, Amanda," she said eventually. "It's wrong, wrong, wrong. The family must be told at once."

"You wouldn't do that to me?" Amanda breathed, as though she didn't think such a thing possible.

"Amanda, you *are* crazy. You just don't know it yet. I can't be party to this massive fraud. If you're frightened Blaine won't give you any money I can speak to him. You were married to Mark. You're entitled. Was this what it was all about at the ski lodge? Mark discovered you were pregnant, and certainly not by him?"

"Whoa!" Amanda yelled. "He didn't know. Mark was eaten up by his own sins."

Sienna felt as if she was descending into her own little hell. "Mandy, let me handle this." She didn't realize she was shaking violently. "We'll say we talked it over and you realized it can't be Mark's baby after all. That you and Mark had as good as broken up. You were desperately unhappy. You turned to someone else for comfort. You're dreadfully sorry for your mistake."

"Prove it." Amanda crossed her arms across her chest in what appeared to be a gesture of triumph.

"Oh, don't be silly!" Sienna burst out, appalled. "There's such a thing as DNA."

Amanda looked back blankly, and then swore. "Don't rat on me, Sienna," she pleaded, her blue eyes like saucers in her white face. "I think I'll kill myself if you do."

Sienna groaned. "I've heard all this talk before. It's called emotional blackmail. You will have your baby. You'll be a rich woman. And I haven't the slightest doubt you'll find someone else." Sienna rose shakily, then walked to the door. "I have to discuss this with Blaine, Amanda. This deception can't go any further."

Amanda rushed to her side. "What if I give you some of it? The money?"

"Ah, *please*." Sienna was filled with despair. "You've landed yourself in a mess, and now we have to get you out of it."

Amanda looked both stricken and amazed. "I'll hate you if you do this," she threatened.

"Hate away. This little plan of yours, Amanda, was never going to work. I can't believe how amoral you've become."

They were out in the gallery now, with Sienna making her way resolutely to the top of the staircase. "Stay there, Amanda. I'll work something out."

"Don't do it. Please don't do it," Amanda implored, her voice rising to a wild shriek. "Sienna!" She had to run to keep up. She was beside herself with panic and rage. Her deception exposed, might she have to suffer the consequences?

No money, when she had already adjusted to the idea of being rich and free of them all?

Sienna cast a hurried look behind her, surprised Amanda was so close on her heels, the expression on her small face near feral. "Go to your room, Mandy," she ordered. "We'll get through this. Leave it to me."

"You?" Amanda exploded, unbalanced by fear and her need for malignant revenge. "I've never been happy. Not a single day of my life. And it's all *your* fault."

The violent accusation hit Sienna like sharp-edged stones hurled in her face. She staggered as Amanda, in a blinding rage, prepared to spring.

It had all come together in Amanda's mind. There would be a kind of justice in sending Sienna hurtling down the stairs.

Only Amanda's high pitched shrieks had brought not only Blaine but Magda, who had been in the kitchen, charging to the scene.

"Sienna—look out!" Blaine roared in a voice like thunder.

Instantly Sienna heeded the warning. She fell back against the timber balustrade, collapsing on the step, while the doll-like Amanda went tumbling down the stairs in her stead.

CHAPTER NINE

Vancouver Island. Three months later.

SIENNA walked along the beach in front of her family retreat, feeling the sun on her head. Water sloshed rhythmically onto the shore, where a jumble of driftwood lay like a piece of sculpture at the water's edge. The house rose up behind her, white weatherboards, tiled roof—a substantial holiday home with a large extension that she and her father used as a studio. The house had breathtaking views of the ocean. They had their own sandstone beach. She had been coming here since she was a child. She loved the place. She had always been happy here. Her mother's father had bought the beautiful peaceful property long ago. It even had mooring for their boat, a yellow kayak, which was beached on the jetty.

Things had changed quite a bit over the years.

The islands were easily accessible by ferry, private boat and plane. She could walk to the shops, the galleries, and to the other amenities if she had a mind. Only she didn't. She was in retreat. She had come to the island to try to recover from an experience that still rocked her.

She and Amanda had left Katajangga in what she thought of as a cloud of disgrace. She felt she would be tainted by it for ever, although that was an irrational judgement. Her mother and father had been waiting for them when they touched down in Vancouver. Her parents had been as appalled as she by Amanda's multiple deceptions and her father had taken charge of Amanda in no uncertain fashion. Amanda had been admitted to a private and very expensive psychiatric clinic to undergo treatment.

In a matter of weeks Amanda had convinced the psychiatrist in attendance she was as sane as the next person. A week later, without a word to anyone, she had taken off for New York. She had money now. She no longer needed the family who had reared her.

"Good riddance!" her mother had said, totally

fed up. "To think she could have killed you, my darling! I don't see how they let her go."

Amanda was a marvellous actress. That was the answer.

Sienna was finishing off a painting in the studio when she heard footsteps on the gravelled section of the rear courtyard.

She put down her paintbrush, wiped her hands on her smock and hurried outdoors. "Hello? Who's there?" She felt no sense of alarm, although the house was very private. At her call, a tall, lean figure came into view. He was dressed in jeans, a blue T-shirt, and a bomber jacket with one side flapping in the breeze.

Blaine.

She couldn't believe it. He had to be a figment of her imagination. She had never stopped thinking about him from the moment they had said a wretched goodbye. She had heard from him, of course, Marcia too—until she had taken refuge from the world on the island. He haunted her, following her wherever she went. She even took him into her bed.

Now the sudden shift from the shade of the

studio to full sun had her blinking, covering her eyes with her hand. For a moment she was mute with astonished joy. "Blaine?" A tremendous excitement descended on her, though she tried to calm herself. He wasn't exactly looking ecstatic to see her.

"Oh, good—you recognize me," he said.

The same vibrant voice. The same clipped tone. The same brilliant eyes. She drew in a great gulp of air. "How did you find me?"

"You *knew* I would." He covered the distance between them, staring down at her, studying her intently. "Your father and I have had a number of fruitful conversations. I've spoken to your mother as well. The only person who has made herself unavailable is *you*."

"I'm sorry. Sorry." She hung her head as Amanda's guilt rippled over her afresh.

"Apologies won't do," he said. "Incidentally, your dad told me what *you* failed to. You covered for Amanda right to the end. Why did you do that?'

"Shame," she confessed, a tremor in her voice. "I don't know to this day if Amanda genuinely believed she was pregnant. I was as shocked as you when the doctor told us she wasn't."

"She was conspiring to rob me, Sienna," he said. "That's the brutal truth. A baby meant lots more money."

"You gave her enough," she said, still keeping her eyes lowered.

"Anything to get rid of her. She had it all planned, Sienna. She almost pulled it off. Knowing what I know now, it was detestable of her to pretend she was carrying Mark's child. Even if she believed herself pregnant—which I doubt—it was another man's."

"Dad shouldn't have told you..." She let her voice trail off.

"Your father was right to tell me," he said forcefully. "We understand why you kept quiet."

She threw up her head. "It would only have caused more pain. I was so upset I just wanted to disappear with my awful delusional cousin. Call it irrational, but I felt I shared the guilt and the shame."

"*Your* only crime, Sienna, was loyalty and the desire not to inflict more hurt. But you could have told *me*. You should have told *me*."

"I know. I wanted to. But I could see Hilary had her doubts about me by the time we got Amanda back from the hospital. If you hadn't broken her fall she could have been badly injured."

"She was quite prepared to injure *you*," he said, showing a flash of anger.

No way to deny it. Amanda *had* meant her harm. "Well, she's taken the money and headed off for New York," she offered very quietly.

"Bless her," said Blaine. "Your dad told me. May we never hear from her again."

"I think I can say amen to that." Her spirits picked up. "Please, Blaine, come into the house," she begged.

"You've been working?" He looked past her into the studio. She was still wearing a paint-splattered smock. "May I see?"

"Of course." She led the way in. Two of her paintings, large-scale botanicals, oil on canvas, were complete. The other, unfinished, sat on the easel.

A look of open admiration broke slowly across Blaine's handsome, dynamic face. "These are really beautiful, Sienna," he said.

"I was searching for something to remind me,"

she explained, struggling not to reach out and touch him.

"Were you, indeed? It's wonderful what you can do." He made his voice casual when he was all heat and fire. "Tell me. Have you missed me?"

Her face revealed what was in her heart. "I've missed you so much you can have no idea."

"Really? I'm amazed." In a moment Blaine knew all would be motion. His whole body was quaking with his need for her. But for now he valiantly held off.

He continued to study her amazing paintings. The Outback flowers he'd been used to all his life had been treated with a kind of passion. Fantastic huge-scale pink waterlilies grew out of one canvas; an extraordinary representation of dozens of floating blood-red Desert Pea glowed richly from another. The unfinished canvas was of a young woman, clearly Sienna, with long flowing amber hair and wearing a gauzy yellow dress. She stood waist-high in a shimmering wonderland of white and yellow paper daisies. The size of the wild flowers, perfect in botanical detail, had been blown up into fantastic blooms that rose all around her and bathed her in radiance.

"I love you." Sienna broke the silence. "I really love you." She had no choice but to tell him. "I can't explain what I've done, but I love you. I—"

Her attempted explanation was cut off. His muscled arms were around her, his hunger for her fully unleashed. "And being with you is the closest I'll ever get to heaven," he rasped. His mouth covered hers with insatiable yearning. "I love you. I *love* you," he muttered, without once breaking the passionate lock of their lips.

Gradually the fierce, needy pressure eased into a deeply desirous exploration that had her moaning and arching her throat. Eventually he picked her up, feeling her long slender legs close convulsively around him.

"Which way's the bedroom?" he groaned. "Though I don't think we can get there." His eyes lit on the big leather chesterfield.

Their clothes evaporated, as though their flesh was so *hot* they couldn't bear to have anything touch their skin.

He held her head, staring into her warm golden eyes. "You can't do this to me again. Understand?"

"I knew you'd find me," she said. "I carried the

thought of it every day. It kept me going. Helped me to paint. *Blaine will come for me.*"

"I'd come for you if you were holed up in an igloo at the North Pole. But don't think for one moment I'm not mad at you."

"You're right to be—yet you're here. I love you," she said all over again. "I can't say it enough times."

"You can try." His hands covered her swelling breasts, and his mouth descended to take in one rosy budded nipple after the other.

The rapture was immense. She moaned as his hand moved down over the flat plane of her stomach, his fingers seeking and then moving into the cleft of her.

She cried out his name, her voice ragged with desire. Her hands were tracing his wide shoulders, moving down his back. He was a dark tan all over, suggesting he had often swum in Katajangga's lagoons naked. His male body was splendid in its form. She spread her legs wide, her bright head rolling from side to side as he entered her. Her hands curved and clawed around him as she fitted herself to him. She couldn't tell where he started and she began. They were gloriously *one.*

I am with him. He is with me.

Sienna had never felt more loved or more safe in her life.

My soul mate has come to get me.

* * * * *

Mills & Boon® Large Print
November 2011

THE MARRIAGE BETRAYAL
Lynne Graham

THE ICE PRINCE
Sandra Marton

DOUKAKIS'S APPRENTICE
Sarah Morgan

SURRENDER TO THE PAST
Carole Mortimer

HER OUTBACK COMMANDER
Margaret Way

A KISS TO SEAL THE DEAL
Nikki Logan

BABY ON THE RANCH
Susan Meier

GIRL IN A VINTAGE DRESS
Nicola Marsh